"I am your mistress."

"Why not?" he asked in a low, furious tone. "What do you want? Marriage?" And when she didn't answer, he carried on relentlessly. "Marriage is not for me."

"And children?" Lisa flung at him.

"...are for other people, and good luck to them. I am offering you as much commitment as I've ever offered any woman. Take it!"

She could feel his eyes burning into her, but she refused to meet them. Did he expect her to abandon everything so she could spend an indefinite length of time living on a knife's edge...?

FROM HERE TO PATERNITY—romances that feature fantastic men who *eventually* make fabulous fathers. Some seek paternity, some have it thrust upon them, all will make it—whether they like it or not!

CATHY WILLIAMS is Trinidadian and was brought up on the twin islands of Trinidad and Tobago. She was awarded a scholarship to study in Britain, and went to Exeter University in 1975 to continue her studies into the great loves of her life: languages and literature. It was there that Cathy met her husband, Richard. Since they married, Cathy has lived in England, originally in the Thames Valley but now in the Midlands. Cathy and Richard have three small daughters.

Books by Cathy Williams

HARLEQUIN PRESENTS
1413—A POWERFUL ATTRACTION
1502—CARIBBEAN DESIRE
1829—BEYOND ALL REASON

Don't miss any of our special offers. Write to us at the following address for information on our newest releases.

Harlequin Reader Service
U.S.: 3010 Walden Ave., P.O. Box 1325, Buffalo, NY 14269
Canadian: P.O. Box 609, Fort Erie, Ont. L2A 5X3

CATHY WILLIAMS

Accidental Mistress

Harlequin Books

TORONTO • NEW YORK • LONDON
AMSTERDAM • PARIS • SYDNEY • HAMBURG
STOCKHOLM • ATHENS • TOKYO • MILAN
MADRID • WARSAW • BUDAPEST • AUCKLAND

If you purchased this book without a cover you should be aware
that this book is stolen property. It was reported as "unsold and
destroyed" to the publisher, and neither the author nor the
publisher has received any payment for this "stripped book."

ISBN 0-373-11909-7

ACCIDENTAL MISTRESS

First North American Publication 1997.

Copyright © 1997 by Cathy Williams.

All rights reserved. Except for use in any review, the reproduction or
utilization of this work in whole or in part in any form by any electronic,
mechanical or other means, now known or hereafter invented, including
xerography, photocopying and recording, or in any information storage
or retrieval system, is forbidden without the written permission of the
publisher, Harlequin Enterprises Limited, 225 Duncan Mill Road,
Don Mills, Ontario, Canada M3B 3K9.

All characters in this book have no existence outside the imagination of
the author and have no relation whatsoever to anyone bearing the same
name or names. They are not even distantly inspired by any individual
known or unknown to the author, and all incidents are pure invention.

This edition published by arrangement with Harlequin Books S.A.

® and TM are trademarks of the publisher. Trademarks indicated with
® are registered in the United States Patent and Trademark Office, the
Canadian Trade Marks Office and in other countries.

Printed in U.S.A.

CHAPTER ONE

IT WAS raining very hard. Lisa Freeman pulled her coat tightly around her, wishing that she had had the sense to wear something waterproof instead of her thick navy blue coat which now seemed to be soaking up every wretched drop of water and growing heavier by the minute.

She also wished that she had had the sense to take a taxi to the airport instead of foolishly counting her pennies and deciding in favour of the bus, because the bus had been running late, so that she had spent the entire journey agonisingly looking at her watch every five minutes to make sure that she wouldn't miss the plane. It had also deposited her further away from the terminal than she had expected, which had meant braving the rain with no hat, no raincoat, one suitcase and her hand luggage.

She dumped the suitcase on the pavement so that she could consult her watch for the millionth time and also give her arm a rest, and comforted herself with the thought that soon she would be flying away from all this appalling weather. Flying to sunny climes—or at least it would be sunny if the newspaper weather listings were anything to go by. Spain, she had read the day before, was warm. Not hot, because it was, after all, January, but warmer than wretched England with its never-ending clouds and wind and sleet and rain and depressing promises of more to come.

Through the driving rain, the airport terminal loomed

in front of her, and she began to feel a little panicky. It was the first time she had ever been overseas. It was difficult to try and think back to exactly when she had started contemplating a holiday abroad. Certainly, as a child, she never had. Her time had been spent on the road, traipsing behind her parents as her father went from one job to another, settling down in cheap rented accommodation, only to be uprooted just when their lives appeared to be taking shape.

It wasn't something that she had resented—at least not until she was old enough to realise that friends would never be a permanent fixture and that the only company she could rely on was her own.

Both her parents were now dead, but the legacy of the nomadic childhood they had subjected her to must have been more tenacious than she would ever have believed possible, because only within the last three years had that ferocious desire to be in one place, to be safe and secure, eased up sufficiently to allow daydreams of other countries to enter her head.

And until now, at the ripe old age of twenty-four, and in an era of cheap foreign travel, she had still never managed to get around to going anywhere out of the country because there had always seemed to be something better to spend her hard-earned money on.

Every year, for the past three years, she'd told herself that she would treat herself, every year she'd religiously collected a mouth-watering pile of brochures on places ranging from the Mediterranean to the Seychelles, every year she'd given herself a long, persuasive lecture on how much she would dearly love a break abroad, and every year she'd worked out the costs.

It had never been feasible. Anywhere like the Seychelles was out of the question. She'd only got the brochures because the pictures were so alluring. And the Mediterranean, while within the scope of her finances—just—had always been so carefully considered, each pro and con meticulously worked out, that in the end she'd always abandoned the idea. The spot of decorating in the living room surely needed doing before a two-week fling on the Costa del Sol. Then there was her car.

Her car, for the past three years, had always seemed to need some expensive repair work just when her savings had reached their optimum in the building society. She had begun to suspect that the heap of slowly disintegrating machinery had a mind of its own and the mind was telling it to make sure that its driver did not vacation abroad and leave it unused for two weeks.

But this time things had worked out for her.

She heaved the suitcase off the pavement, realising that it felt even heavier now that she had rested her arm for a few minutes, and thought about that envelope that had slipped into her letterbox three months before.

Never having won anything in her life before, and then suddenly winning a trip abroad had made it doubly exciting.

She smiled at the memory of it, stepped off the pavement with her eyes firmly focused on the terminal building ahead of her, which, through the driving rain, was only a blurred outline, and then what happened next became a somewhat confused sequence of events.

Had she slipped on the wet road? Had she stupidly not looked where she was going? Or had the driver of the car been as blinded by the rain as she had?

She just knew that she saw the car bearing down on her, moving quite slowly, although from where she was standing it seemed like a hundred miles an hour, at precisely the same time as the driver saw her step in front of it. There was a horrendous squeal of brakes and she felt a sharp burst of pain as the car swerved, but not enough to stop it from glancing against her leg.

She lay on the ground, unable to move, and all she could think was that she was going to miss her holiday. She had spent every waking hour looking forward to it and now she was going to miss it. She didn't even stop to think that she was lucky—that things could have been worse.

Her leg was hurting badly, with a red-hot pain that made her grit her teeth, and in between the pain she had images of the plane taking off and merrily winging its way to sunny climes without her, and depositing all of its passengers onto the tarmac at the other end, less one, because here she was, lying on the ground, with what felt very much like a broken leg. Or at any rate a leg that wasn't going to do much walking for a little while yet.

She moaned heavily, noticing that quite a crowd appeared to have gathered around her and also that her suitcase had thoughtfully split open and was revealing its cargo of sodden clothes to whoever cared to look.

'I've called an ambulance from my car phone,' a voice said from next to her and she turned her head slowly towards it. 'It will be here any minute.'

The onlookers were crowding in to hear what was said, and the man, whoever he was, made a swift, authoritative movement with his hand. They shuffled back and within a few minutes most of them had dispersed.

Lisa looked at him. He had black hair, plastered against his face because of the rain, although that didn't appear to bother him unduly, and the lines of his face were harsh and aggressive. Aggressive enough to have sent the circle of bystanders skittering away.

He looked down at her and the fuzzy, fleeting impression of someone quite good-looking crystallised into the most amazingly masculine face she had ever seen in her life. His features were hard, his eyes startlingly blue, the face of a man born to give orders.

'Are you an airport official?' she asked faintly, and a glimmer of a smile curved his mouth.

'Do I resemble an airport official?' he asked. He had a nice voice, she thought, deep, lazy, with an undertone of amusement running through it that lent it a certain indefinable charm.

She heard the wail of the ambulance pelting towards them.

'I hope it stops in time,' she said with weak humour, no longer thinking of the missed holiday, simply relieved that she would soon be able to have some wonderful, numbing injection to take the pain away, 'or else there will be a few more broken bodies lying around than they'd bargained for.'

The man, who was still bending over her and was not an airport official—stupid question really since she could see his expensive grey suit underneath the flaps of his overcoat and since when did airport officials wear expensive grey suits?—laughed. He had, she thought, closing her eyes and feeling rather light-headed and faint, a rather nice laugh as well. Warm and rich and vaguely unsettling. Or maybe the pain was just making her hallucinate slightly.

Then, through the swimming haze, she heard voices and the sounds of things happening and she felt someone carefully examining her, feeling her leg—but so skilfully that it didn't hurt—and then everything moved quickly.

Painkillers were administered, she was carried by stretcher into the back of the ambulance, still with her eyes closed, and that was all she remembered.

The next time she opened her eyes she was on a small bed, in a small room, with a doctor bending over her and a thermometer sticking sideways out of her mouth.

'I'm Dr Sullivan,' the man said, smiling, while the nurse who was standing next to the bed whipped the thermometer out of her mouth, looked at it, and then shook it so vigorously that Lisa, staring, felt quite faint. 'Do you remember how you got here?'

She dragged her attention away from the nurse, now writing up some notes. 'Hit by a car,' she said with a faint smile. While clutching my battered suitcase, she could have added, and feeling terribly thrilled at the prospect of a holiday abroad.

'You've suffered a fracture to your leg,' the doctor said, 'and quite a few bruises which will look far worse than they feel. I need not tell you that you were very lucky indeed.'

'I would feel luckier if it hadn't happened in the first place,' Lisa said seriously, and the young doctor threw her a bemused look before smiling politely.

'Of course you would, my dear,' he said kindly, straightening up and consulting his watch. 'But unfortunately these things happen. It does mean, however, that you'll be with us for a couple of weeks, while everything knits back together. Nurse will show you where everything is, and I shall be back to have a look at you later on today.'

Nurse was smiling efficiently and as soon as the doctor had left she fussed around the bed, pointing out where the alarm call was, the light switch, the television switch, and then she said, as she was leaving, 'You have a visitor, by the way.'

'A visitor? What visitor?'

The nurse smiled coyly, which only served to deepen Lisa's bewilderment.

'I thought he was your young man, actually. He travelled behind the ambulance to the hospital and he's been waiting here ever since.'

Lisa would have liked to ask a few more questions, including what had happened to her suitcase, last seen baring its contents to all and sundry, but the nurse was already leaving and in her place walked the man who had been bending over her on the road. Her visitor. The man with no name who had taken control of everything until the ambulance had arrived.

She looked at him as he shut the door quietly behind him and felt a quiver of pleasure surge through her. She also felt quite surprisingly shy and tongue-tied and she had to make a huge effort to tell herself that she was being silly.

She was a grown woman now. No longer the child trailing behind her parents, no longer the gauche adolescent with no experience of the opposite sex, no longer the young girl deprived of that network of giggling contemporaries who dropped her eyes and pulled away the minute a boy started taking an interest in her. Those years were behind her now. She told herself that quite firmly and felt better.

She furtively eyed her visitor as he pulled the one and only chair over to her bed, sat down, and proceeded to give her the full benefit of his attention.

'I believe the last time we spoke no introductions were made,' he said, and his voice was precisely as she remembered. Dark and somehow inviting you to give all your attention back to him. Willing it, in fact. 'How are you feeling?'

He had dried out. His hair, she saw now, was thick and black, as were his eyelashes, and he had removed his coat and jacket and rolled the sleeves of his white shirt up to the elbows, so that she could see his forearms, with their sprinkling of fine dark hair.

'Fine,' she said. 'A bit restricted, but I suppose I'll get used to that in due course.'

'I'm Angus Hamilton, by the way,' he said with a smile, stretching out his hand to her and then grasping hers so that she felt her skin tingle, and she hurriedly shoved it away under the starched sheet as soon as she could.

'Lisa Freeman,' she said, blushing slightly. 'Nurse said that you came here after the accident. There was no need, really.'

'Oh, but there was every need.' He sat back in the chair, which seemed far too small to accommodate him. 'You see, it was my driver who knocked you over. I'm afraid he didn't see you soon enough. You stepped out in front of the car and he tried to brake in time. The rest is history.' He was looking at her intently as he said all this, his blue eyes fixed on her face.

'Oh.' She paused. 'I should have used the pedestrian crossing,' she said frankly. 'I was in a dreadful rush, though.' She thought about the wonderful holiday and her frantic preparations and felt a lump of regret swell in her throat. 'What happened to my suitcase?'

'I collected the lot and gave it to the nurse. Were you on your way to catch a plane?'

'Lanzarote.' She was normally quite a self-contained person but right now she felt emotional, with tears brimming up behind her eyes.

'I'm really very sorry,' he said, and to her embarrassment he reached into his pocket and extracted a fresh white handkerchief which he handed to her. 'I have no idea what happens in a situation like this, but I'm sure that some compensation can be reached. I've sorted out this room for you and naturally I shall make sure that whatever money has been lost on your holiday is forwarded to you.'

'Y-you sorted out this room?' Lisa repeated, stammering.

'Your stay here will be private.'

'There was no need.' She looked at him, aghast. It had crossed her mind that being the sole occupant in a room in a very busy hospital was a bit peculiar, but it had never occurred to her that someone else might have paid for it.

'It was the least I could do,' he said, frowning.

'Well, it's enough.' She looked at him firmly. 'I can't possibly ask you for any kind of financial compensation for an accident that was partly my fault and partly the fault of the heavens opening up.' In fact, thinking about it, it was probably more her fault than the fault of the weather because she hadn't been looking where she was going. She had stepped out from between two parked cars, intent on getting to that terminal before her arms gave out completely.

'Don't be a fool,' he told her, but sounded more perplexed and irritated than angry.

'I'm not. I don't want any money from you.'

'And what about your holiday?'

Lisa shrugged and pictured herself lying by a pool somewhere with a tinge of regret. 'It was too good to be true anyway,' she said on a sigh. 'I won it, you see.

I entered a competition in a magazine and won it, so it's not really as though I've lost any money or anything.'

'You won it?' He made it sound as though having to enter competitions to get holidays was something utterly unheard of and she said, defensively,

'I can't afford one otherwise!'

She looked at him properly, not at his physical appearance, but at his clothes, his shoes, his watch, and she realised that, although she had no idea what he did for a living, whatever it was paid well because he exuded that air of confidence and power that came to people who had a great deal of wealth. Not the sort of man that she would ever have met under normal circumstances, nor the sort that she would have wanted to meet. A man destined to lead women up garden paths. From the pinnacle of inexperience, she felt sure that she had summed him up correctly.

'Which is all the more reason...'

'On no condition will I accept money from you! I was in the wrong and I would have a guilty conscience if I felt that I had swindled you out of money.'

'I can afford it, for heaven's sake!' He was beginning to look as though she had taken leave of her senses. 'You're not swindling me out of anything!'

'No.'

'Are you always so stubborn?' he asked, with a faintly mystified look. 'I must say it's a new experience to want to give money away only to find it flung back in my face.'

He gave her a long, slow smile that was so full of unintentional charm that she felt her head begin to swim a little. Had she ever met a man as potent as this one was? she wondered. Was that why he was having this heady effect on her? Maybe the fact that she was stuffed full of painkillers had something to do with it. All that medication would have thrown her system out of focus, might be making her responses go awry. She blinked and looked at him and still felt as though something tight was gripping her chest.

'Do you work?' he asked at last, curiously. 'Does it not pay enough for you to have a holiday now and again? When was the last time you had a holiday?'

'I might be stubborn,' Lisa said tartly, 'but at least I'm not nosy.'

'Everyone's nosy,' Angus said, looking at her with a mixture of curiosity and amusement.

'Oh, are they? What a strange world you must live in, where everyone's nosy and willing to accept money wherever it comes from and whatever the circumstances.'

He looked even more vastly amused by that and she felt the colour crawl up into her face, making her hot and addled. For a second she was the fourteen-year-old girl in her party frock again, anxiously waiting at the front door for her first date to arrive, hoping that he wouldn't notice the packing cases, still only half-unpacked in the small living room, assured by her parents that she looked lovely, but knowing deep down that she just looked plain and unexciting. She was only ever exciting in her mind. In reality, she knew that she was shy and reserved and that any self-confidence she had acquired over the years was really only a thin veneer.

'I hope you're not laughing at me,' she said now.

'Laughing at you?' His dark eyebrows shot up. 'Someone with such admirable principles?'

He *was* laughing at her. He was thinking that she was gauche and ingenuous and naïve and heaven only knew what else besides.

'Well,' she said, trying to sound composed, 'in answer to your questions, yes, I have got a job, yes, I suppose I could just afford to go abroad now and again—well, once a year, anyway—but something would suffer, and as a matter of fact I have never been on a holiday.'

'You have never been on a holiday?' He sounded incredulous and she glared at him defensively.

'That's right,' she snapped. 'Is it so unheard of?'

'Largely speaking, yes,' he answered bluntly. He was looking at her as though he had come across a strange species of creature, believed extinct, which, against her better judgement, made her stammer out an explanation of sorts.

'M-my parents travelled around the country a lot... My father didn't...didn't like to be in one place for too long...nor Mum... They—they liked the feeling of being on the move, you see...'

'How thoughtful of them, considering they had a child. Are you an only child? Have you any sisters? Brothers?'

'No. And my parents were wonderful!' she said hotly. True enough, they had been thoughtless—a conclusion she had arrived at for herself a long time ago—but in a vague, generous way. Was it their fault that she had come along? Out of the blue when her parents were already in their early forties?

'And now your one opportunity lands you up in hospital.' He shook his head ruefully, swerving off the subject with such expertise that she was almost taken aback.

'I think fate is trying to tell me something,' she conceded with a little laugh.

Outside, night had fallen, black, cold, starless. The bright, fluorescent overhead bulb threw his face into startling contrast, accentuating his perfectly chiselled features. She wondered how she looked. The doctor had said that she had a few bruises, which probably meant that her face was every colour of the rainbow, and her hair, which had dried, would look straggly and unkempt.

For a moment she felt a burning sense of embarrassment. It was a bit like bouncing into your favourite film star on the one day of the year when you hadn't put on any make-up and were suffering from a bad cold.

She couldn't remember the last time she had been bothered by her looks—or rather her lack of them. She had stopped looking into mirrors and wistfully longing to see a tall, big-busted blonde looking back at her. She had come through that awkward, insecure adolescence and had emerged a sensible, down-to-earth woman who could handle most situations.

Now, though, lying here on the hospital bed, Lisa felt plain. Too pale, too fine-featured ever to be labelled earthy or voluptuous, hair too brown, without any interesting highlights, breasts too small.

'Where exactly do you work?' he asked.

'Are you really interested? You mustn't feel that you've got to be kind or that you've got to stay here with me for an appropriate length of time.'

'Stubborn,' he drawled, leaning back in the chair and folding his hands behind his head, 'and argumentative.'

Argumentative? Her? When was the last time she had argued with anyone? Not for years. She had always been quite happy to leave the arguing to the rest of the world.

'I am neither stubborn nor argumentative,' she defended heatedly, then smiled a little sheepishly because her tone belied the statement. 'I just wouldn't like you to feel that you should stay here and chat to me simply because your driver knocked me over.'

'I never do anything unless I want to,' he said matter-of-factly. 'I certainly do not profess interest in people unless I am genuinely interested in them.'

'In that case, I work at a nursery.'

'Lots of screaming children?' He didn't look as though the idea of that was in the slightest appealing and she wondered again about his lifestyle. She had never even thought to ask herself whether he was married or not. Somehow, he didn't give the impression of being a married man. Too hard, perhaps, too single-minded. Certainly, if his expression was anything to go by, he didn't have much to do with children and he liked it that way.

'Not all children scream,' Lisa pointed out reasonably. 'And when they do there's usually a cause. Anyway, I work at a garden centre—Arden Nurseries, if you must know.'

She would have to ring Paul and tell him what had happened. He would be as disappointed as she was. He had been thrilled when she had won the holiday. He was always telling her that she worked too hard, but in fact she enjoyed it. She loved plants and flowers. If she hadn't left school at seventeen to enter the workforce, she would perhaps have stayed on and studied botany at university.

'And where do you work?' she asked.

'An advertising firm,' he said. 'Hamilton Scott.'

'How interesting.' She smiled politely. 'And what do you do there?'

'Are you really interested?' he asked, mimicking her. 'You needn't feel that you've got to ask.' He laughed and then said, watching her for her reaction, 'You look charming when you blush.'

His vivid blue eyes skimmed over her face and she didn't quite know what to say in response to his observation. This type of lazy, sophisticated flirting—if that was what it was—was beyond her. But then he worked in advertising, the glamour industry, and she worked in a garden centre, spending half her time with her hands covered in soil and compost, wearing dungarees, and with her shoulder-length hair carelessly tied up.

'I own the company,' he said casually. 'My father founded it, ran it down with a handful of spectacularly bad decisions, and since then I have rebuilt it.' He was still smiling, and underneath the smile she could see the glint of ruthlessness, the mark of a man to be feared and respected and courted.

'How nice,' she said, for want of anything better to say, and he laughed aloud at that.

'Isn't it? It doesn't impress you a great deal, though, does it?'

'What doesn't?'

'Me.'

Lisa went bright red and then felt annoyed because there was something deliberately wicked about his teasing, as though she intrigued him, and not because she was sexy, or stimulating, but because she was novel, a type that perhaps he had never encountered before, or at least never to speak to. In short, in his world of twentieth-century glamour and sophistication, she was a dinosaur.

'I am always impressed when people do well,' she said coolly. 'My boss, Paul, started the nursery with a loan from the bank and a desire to work hard, and he made a success of it, and that impresses me as well. But mostly I'm impressed with people for what they are and not what they achieve. A person might have a nice car and live in a grand house and travel in great style, but if he isn't a good person, caring and thoughtful and honest, then what's the point of all the rest?' She meant it, too, although, hearing herself, she realised that she sounded, ever so slightly, as though she was preaching.

'And money means nothing to you?' He lifted his eye-brows fractionally and again she had the impression of being observed with curiosity and interest rather than the magnetic pull of attraction.

'Only in so far as I have enough to get by.'

'And you don't yearn for more?'

'No. I presume, though, that you do?'

'Not more money, no,' he said slowly, as though the question had never been put to him before. 'I have more than enough of that. What I find stimulating is to scale the heights I have imposed on myself.' He paused and then asked, changing the subject, which was a bit of a shame, because she had found herself hanging onto his every word, spellbound by his personality even if the feeling wasn't mutual, 'How long will you be in here?'

'About two weeks,' she answered. 'With any luck, less. I would prefer to convalesce at home.'

'And you have someone there to look after you? A boyfriend perhaps?' The half-closed blue eyes watched her in a way that made her want to fidget.

'Oh, no,' she said airily, 'not at the moment.' Imply-ing that she was sort of resting in between bouts of heavy romance, which was so far from the truth that it was almost laughable.

Robert, her last boyfriend, had worked in a car firm and had wanted marriage, a terraced house, two point four children and steak every Friday. She had been ap-palled at the prospect and had broken it off, but since stability was what he had been offering and stability was what she had always desperately wanted she had been puzzled at her immediate response when it had been offered. A break, she had thought then, will do me good. That had been two years ago and the break now seemed to be of a more permanent nature than she had originally intended.

'My friend lives just around the corner, but I can manage on my own anyway.'

'Can you?'

'Of course I can,' she said, surprised. 'I always have.'

'Yes.' He looked at her thoughtfully. 'I expect you have.' He stood up and began rolling down his sleeves, before slipping on his jacket and thrusting his hands in the pockets. 'I find that rather sad, though.'

'Don't feel sorry for me,' Lisa said rather more acidly than she had intended. She shrugged. 'It's a fact of life. It's important to know how to stand on your own two feet.'

'Do you really believe that or is that the consolation prize for a life spent on the road?'

She flushed and looked away.

'Not that that's any of my business.' His voice was gentler as he smiled and said, again, how sorry he was about what had happened. He handed her his card, plain white with his name printed on it, and the name of his company, and his fax number as well as three more work numbers, and an intricate abstract design at the bottom which she thought probably meant something, though what she couldn't think.

'Call me if you change your mind about the compensation I'm more than willing to give you,' he said, and stopped her before she could open her mouth and inform him that she wasn't about to change her mind. 'Money might well mean nothing to you, but after this you could do with a good holiday somewhere and I would be happy to pay for it.'

'All right,' she said, propping the card against the glass of water on the table next to her.

'But you have no intention of availing yourself of the offer…'

'None whatsoever,' Lisa agreed, and he shook his head wryly.

He walked over to the door and then paused.

'I'm away for the next ten days,' he said, 'or else I would come and look in, and please don't tell me that there's no need or I'll wring your neck.'

'I don't think I could cope with a sore neck and a fractured leg as well,' she said, smiling. He had only been with her half an hour, if that, but seeing him standing there, with his hand on the doorknob, his body already half turned to leave, she felt a sudden, inexplicable pang which surprised and disoriented her.

She couldn't possibly want him to stay, could she? she wondered. Wouldn't that be altogether pathetic when he had come on what was, essentially, a courtesy visit? She should never have told him all that stuff about her parents. She seldom shared confidences, least of all with a stranger, and now she felt as though he was walking off with a little bit of her tucked away with him, and she didn't like the feeling.

'Goodbye, Lisa Freeman,' he said. 'You're really rather a remarkable girl.'

'Goodbye, Angus Hamilton,' she replied, and when she tried to add a witty comment to that, as he had, nothing came out. She just continued smiling as he closed the door behind him, and then she pictured him striding along the hospital corridor, gathering admiring glances from all the nurses and female patients, walking purposefully towards his car, ready to be chauffeured back to his apartment or house or mansion or wherever it was he lived, because she hadn't the faintest idea.

The mental scenario so overtook the thought of lying by a non-existent pool in the sunshine that, after a while, she shook herself and wondered whether perhaps she was missing the company of a man in her life rather more than she had consciously thought.

She had her little flat, a modern, one-bedroom place on a nicely kept estate a few miles from the nursery, so that travelling to and from work wasn't too hazardous a prospect in her unreliable Mini. She had her friends, most of whom lived locally, and she carefully tended those relationships because in a world with no family friends became your only standby. She especially treasured them because friendships had been so hard to form as she'd roamed with her parents.

She hadn't felt the absence of a boyfriend in her life. Why, then, had she been so stupidly invigorated by *this* man—someone whom she had never met in her life before, a man who lived in an orbit as far removed from hers as Mars was from the planet Earth?

She hadn't thought that she was lonely, but—who knew?—perhaps she was.

Paul, her boss, had been trying for ages to arrange a blind date between her and his cousin, whose credentials seemed to be that he was a nice chap and supported the same football team as Paul did. Maybe, she thought, buzzing the nurse for some more painkillers because her leg, which had been feeling fine, was now throbbing madly, she would give him a go.

That settled in her mind, she eyed Angus Hamilton's business card and then shoved it inside the drawer of the beside cabinet, where it was safely out of sight and safely out of mind.

Then she got down to the overdue business of ringing her closest friends, who sympathised with her bad luck and promised to visit with magazines and flowers and grapes—what else? She also phoned Paul, who soothed and clucked like a mother hen and told her that there was no need to rush back to work until she was ready, but could she tell him where that number for the delivery firm who were supposed to have delivered some shrubs that morning was, because they hadn't and he intended to give them an earful?

Then she settled down, closed her eyes and spent the night dreaming of Angus Hamilton.

CHAPTER TWO

IT WAS two months before her leg was more or less back in working order. She was confined, by Paul, to doing what he called sitting duties, by which he meant tackling all the paperwork.

'All very restful,' he assured her, then proceeded to produce several box files of papers which were in a rampant state of disorder and left her to it.

But she was busy, and for that she was grateful. Only occasionally did she think about the missed holiday, wondering what it would have been like and promising herself that she would get there. Some time. Possibly even during the summer, although Paul didn't like any of his staff, least of all her because he depended on her, to take their holidays during the busiest months of the year.

Rather too often for comfort, she thought about Angus. She must, she thought, have absorbed a lot of detail about him because he still hadn't conveniently faded into a blurry image. She could still recall quite clearly everything about him, even little nuances which she must have unconsciously observed as he had sat there on the hospital chair talking to her, and stored away at the back of her mind.

She hadn't told a soul about him. Not her friends, not Paul. He was a secret, *her* secret. Instinct told her that to talk about him would give even more substance to his memory.

He wasn't about to reappear in her life, was he? What

was the point of inviting curiosity about someone who
had appeared and vanished as quickly as a dream?

She was so utterly convinced of this that when, nearly
three months after she had last seen him and weeks after
she had joyfully relegated her waking stick to the broom
cupboard under the stairs of her flat, she found his letter
lying on her doormat she was so shocked that she felt
her breathing become heavy and her hands begin to per-
spire.

She knew who the letter was from even before she
ripped open the envelope. The writing was firm, in black
ink, and the postmark was London. Apart from Angus
Hamilton, she knew no one else in London who would
send her a letter.

The message was short and to the point. He was going
on a cruise with a few friends and would she like to
accompany them. 'Of course,' she read, sitting down on
the small sofa in her lounge and tucking her feet underneath her, 'you will not even think of refusing this invitation. Consider it an act of charity on your part to
ease my guilty conscience over the accident.' As a post-
script, he had added, 'I trust you are now back on both
feet.'

Of course, she had no intention of accepting, never
mind his guilty conscience. She kept the letter in her bag
and pulled it out whenever there was no one around, and
then told herself why she had no intention of accepting
his invitation.

For a start, it just wasn't *her* to rush off and do something like that. Spontaneity was all well and good, but
she had spent so many years being swept along on the
tide of her parents' spontaneity, like a leaf constantly
caught up in a wind storm, that she had come to realise
that thinking things through was a much better alterna-

tive. Thinking things through gave coherence to the whole disordered business of living.

When her parents had died, she had been just seventeen and craving for what most girls her age would have hated: somewhere to call a home, somewhere safe where she could gaze out through the window and watch the seasons change and the years pass, without any plans for moving on. She never wanted impulsiveness to dictate her actions. Never, never, never. It was dangerous.

Then, reluctantly, she remembered his face. She remembered the pity she had glimpsed there when she had told him that she was used to standing on her own two feet. Pity at what he saw as a sad little thing.

Her parents had felt a little sorry for her as well. How could they have produced such a quiet, timid version of themselves, when they were so exuberant? They had never understood that spending a year or eighteen months in one place before moving on to a different place with different faces and different landmarks was something that she had found increasingly disorienting.

So she found herself accepting his invitation. It was as easy as that. Something stronger than common sense, some powerful emotional urge, tipped the scales, almost when she hadn't been looking.

She called the number on the letter, spoke to an efficient-sounding woman who informed her that she was Mr Hamilton's personal assistant, and threw caution to the winds before she could work out all the pros and cons and ifs and buts.

And here I am now, she thought three weeks later, paying the price for a few moments of recklessness. Feeling nervous and sick and apprehensive and knowing that I'm not going to enjoy a minute of this. It will be an ordeal.

The only saving grace was that there would be lots of people around on the liner so if she found the company of Angus and his friends too uncomfortable she could always lose herself in the crowd. No one would think her odd. Cruise liners were always full of solitary women.

She closed her eyes when the plane took off and for an instant she stopped thinking about what lay ahead of her and thought instead about the dynamics of something as heavy as this being able to travel in the air. She hoped that all the nuts and bolts were firmly screwed together and risked a quick look through the window, open-mouthed at the sight of land fast disappearing beneath her, to be replaced by an infinity of sky and clouds.

She hadn't felt nearly so nervous about Lanzarote. She wondered whether the captain would turn back and let her off at Heathrow if she asked nicely. Failing that, she could hop it back to England when they landed at Barbados and Angus Hamilton, with his far-fetched notions of applying a balm to his guilty conscience, would be none the wiser. He would shrug those powerful shoulders of his and get on with his holiday knowing that he had tried to make amends and she had rudely refused.

He probably would not even miss the money he had spent on her airline ticket.

But since she knew, deep down, that she would obey the instructions kindly laid out for her in the letter from his secretary she didn't feel much better.

She arrived at Barbados feeling rather ragged and, as the unknown secretary had helpfully advised in the letter which had accompanied the airline ticket, made her way to the transit desk and eventually onto the connecting flight to St Vincent.

This time the scenery through the window was rather

more spectacular. She left Barbados looking down at glittering blue sea and strips of white sand and landed in St Vincent to the same staggering view.

The taxi driver was waiting outside the airport for her—just as the secretary had said he would be—when she emerged with her suitcase and her holdall.

She had worn a loose, flowery skirt and a short-sleeved shirt, but nothing had prepared her for the heat that hit her the minute she was in the open. It was the sort of all-enveloping heat which she had never before experienced in England, not even when it got very hot during the best of the summer days.

There was a great deal of activity outside the airport, taxi drivers waiting hopefully by their cars to take tourists to their destinations, but there was nothing frenetic about any of it. No one seemed to be in any kind of rush to get anywhere.

'Where are you taking me?' she asked the driver as he cruised off at one mile per hour.

'Not far.' He looked at her in the rear-view mirror, showing two rows of gleaming white teeth. 'The hotel, it just along the south coast. Very nice place.'

Lisa lapsed into silence to contemplate the scenery, leaning forward slightly in her seat with her hands nervously clutching her bag.

Outside, the marvellous vista unfolded itself Everything was so lush and green, heavy with the scent of the Tropics. She half wished that it would go on for ever, partly because it was so beautiful and partly because she was beginning to feel sick and nervous all over again.

What on earth was she going to say to him? She wasn't accustomed to mixing in sophisticated circles. She would be completely at a loss for witty, interesting

topics of discussion. After one hour, she would no longer
be the novelty which had amused him months ago in a
hospital ward. She would revert to being just an ordinary
young woman without much of a talent for being in the
limelight.

The taxi driver pulled up outside the hotel, which appeared to comprise a collection of stone cottages strewn
with well thought out randomness amongst the lush veg-
etation.

He helped her with her luggage and she was almost
sorry to see him depart into the distance, driving away
as slowly as he had arrived.

She looked around her helplessly, noticing with a
sinking heart the other visitors at the hotel who seemed
to waft past her, laughing in their elegant attire. Would
they all be on the liner? she wondered. Was this hotel
one of the stops between ports? She had no idea. She
glanced down at her clothes self-consciously, and when
she raised her eyes to the reception desk there he was,
standing there, just as she remembered him.

He was wearing a pair of light olive-green trousers
and a cream shirt and he was, thankfully, alone.

As he approached her, she noticed how the other fe-
males strolling through the foyer darted glances at him,
as if they couldn't help themselves. 'I thought,' he said,
'that you might back out at the last minute.'

He was taller than she remembered. From a supine
position on a hospital bed, it had been difficult to get a
good idea of his height, but now she could see that he
was over six feet tall, and already bronzed from the sun,
so that his eyes looked bluer and more striking than she
remembered.

'I take it that your leg has now fully recovered from
the experience?' One of the hotel staff hurried up to

gather her luggage and she followed him as he checked her in.

'Yes, it has,' she said to his profile, watching as he smiled and then turned to look at her. 'Thank you very much for...this.' She spread her arms vaguely to encompass everything around her. 'It was very kind of you.'

He was watching her as she said this, with a small smile on his mouth, and it was a relief when the porter interrupted them to show her to her room, which wasn't a room at all, but in fact one of the stone cottages with a thatched roof and a marvellous view overlooking the sea. Blue, blue sea and white, white sand.

'Was your trip all right?'

'Oh, yes, thank you very much; it was fine.'

'There's no need to be quite so terrifyingly polite,' he said, amused.

'I'm sorry. Was I?'

'You were.' He folded his arms and looked at her. 'You haven't been invited along to be thrown to the sharks.'

'No, I know that.' She tried a smile.

'That's better.' He smiled back at her. 'You're here to enjoy yourself. That's why you came, isn't it?'

'Yes, of course.' Her replies sounded stilted and she glanced around her for inspiration.

'I'm surprised that you came at all, I don't mind admitting. After what you had told me at the hospital about not accepting charity, I thought that you'd run a mile at the prospect of a holiday at my expense.'

She resisted the temptation to apologize once again, but his remark filled her with dismay. Had he been banking on her not coming? Was that it?

'I...accepted on impulse,' she admitted, looking down

to where her fingers were twined around the handle of her bag.

'I'm glad to hear it. Now,' he continued briskly, 'I expect you're feeling rather tired. He leaned against the doorframe and stared down at her. 'There's absolutely no need for you to emerge for dinner. They will happily bring you some food here if you'd rather just stay in and recover from the trip. Tomorrow morning we're hoping to set sail.'

'Yes, of course. Your secretary did list the itinerary. I have it here in my bag somewhere.' She plunged nervously into the bowels of the tan bag and several bits of paper fluttered to the ground, accompanied by a half-empty packet of travel tissues, several sweets, her traveller's cheques and her book, of which she had read very little on the plane.

They both bent to recover the dropped items at the same time and their heads bumped. Lisa pulled away in embarrassment, red-faced, cursing the bag, which was much too large really and had somehow managed to attract quite a bit of paraphernalia in a way that her normal tiny one never did.

'S-sorry,' she stammered, burning with confusion as he handed her the packet of tissues and the sweets, which she stuffed back into the bag.

'There's no need to be nervous,' he told her gently, kneeling opposite her.

'I'm not nervous!' She was kneeling too, her hands resting lightly on her thighs, her face close to his in the twilight which seemed to have descended abruptly in the space of about ten minutes. She remembered reading that about the Tropics. There was no lingering dusk. Night succeeded day swiftly.

'Of course you are,' he said, as though surprised that

she could deny the obvious. 'You're going on a fortnight's vacation on a yacht with a group of people whom you've never seen in your life before. Of course you're nervous.'

She sprang up as though burnt and looked at him in confusion.

'Yacht? I thought it was a cruise.'

'Yacht, cruise, where's the difference?' He stood up and frowned. 'Are you all right? You look a bit peculiar.'

'Look,' she said steadily, even though she could feel herself shaking, 'please could you clarify what exactly this holiday is? Are we or are we not going on a liner?'

'Liner? What are you talking about?'

'In your letter, you said that we would be cruising... I was under the impression...'

His face cleared and he laughed. 'That we were going on a cruise ship? No. I think there's been a misunderstanding. No cruise ship. As far as I'm concerned, there wouldn't be much point in getting away from the madding crowd only to surround yourself by the same madding crowd, just with a change of faces. In fact, I can't really think of anything worse; don't you agree?'

No, she wanted to shout in frustrated panic, I most certainly do not agree! And I can think, offhand, of one thing that's infinitely worse. It involves a group of friends, on a yacht, none of whom I know, and *me*!

'I—I would never have come...' she stammered in horror.

'If you'd known? You coward.'

'I really don't think that I can... There's been a mistake... It's not your fault... I should have asked, but I didn't think... I'm sorry, but...'

'Don't be foolish.'

'I am not being foolish!' Now she was beginning to feel angry as well as horrified.

'Look at me.'

She did. Reluctantly.

'Do I look like someone who is thoughtless enough to invite you out here, throw you into the deep end and watch you struggle with a smile on my face?'

Pretty much, she thought to herself.

'No, no, I'm sure you're not, but really…I don't relish the thought of… I shall be an intrusion…' Her voice was beginning to fail her under the sheer horror of the enormous misunderstanding that had landed her out here, a million miles away from home, like a stranded fish out of water. She tried to remind herself that she was capable of enormous self-control, a legacy of having spent much of her childhood living in her own world, but something about his commanding, powerful presence made it difficult.

'Nonsense. An intrusion into what?' He didn't give her time to answer. 'Let me have the key. It's ludicrous to be standing out here having a lengthy discussion when we could be inside.'

She handed him the key and barely glanced around her as they entered.

'An intrusion into your privacy,' she explained in a high voice that bordered on the desperate. 'You will be with your friends…'

'What do you think of the cottage?' He turned around from where he had been standing by one of the windows, looking out into the black velvet night, and faced her.

'Super. Wonderful,' she said miserably.

'You've never had a holiday in your life before, Lisa.' His voice was soothing and gentle, the voice of someone dealing with a child, a child whose wits were just a little scrambled, and who needed to be taken by the hand and pointed in the right direction. 'You told me so yourself. When I booked this holiday, I thought about that. Why don't you put aside your reservations for a moment and try and see the next two weeks for what they are? An eye-opener.'

'You invited me along because you felt sorry for me.' She spoke flatly, acknowledging the suspicion which had been there at the back of her mind from the beginning.

He shrugged and stuck his hands into his pockets.

'That's putting it a little strongly.'

'But basically that's it, isn't it?' She could feel tears of anger and humiliation springing to her eyes and she tightened her mouth.

'I felt that I owed you something for having deprived you of a holiday abroad. I wouldn't call that a crime, would you?'

He had a seductive way of talking. Great intelligence and great charm could be a persuasive combination. She sighed and suddenly felt overwhelmingly tired.

'Not a crime, no. But you must understand that...'

'You're apprehensive.'

'I wish you'd stop finishing my sentences for me,' she said crossly. 'I'm quite capable of finishing them myself.'

He smiled, not taking his eyes off her. 'You're scared stiff at the thought of mixing with a group of people you've never met in your life before.'

'Wouldn't *you* be?' she flung at him.

'No.'

'Well, excuse me while I just fetch out my medal for bravery from my bag!' she snapped, and he moved towards her, which she found, inexplicably, so alarming that she had to make an effort not to retreat to the furthest corner of the room.

'That's much better,' he drawled, standing in front of her.

'What's much better?'

'A bit of fire instead of passively assuming the worst before you've even tested the water. Now, tomorrow,' he continued, before she could think that out. 'We normally breakfast in our rooms. Less effort than trying to arrange a time to meet in the restaurant area. We're going to meet at the yacht at twelve-thirty. Shall we come and collect you or would you rather have a look around here and make your way to the boat yourself?'

'How many will there be?' she asked, frowning.

'Just six of us. One of my clients who also happens to be a close personal friend, his wife and their daughter, and a cousin of sorts.'

'A cousin of sorts?'

'We're related somewhere along the line but so distantly that it would take for ever trying to work the link out.'

'Oh.'

'And you still haven't answered my question.'

'Question? What question?'

He grinned with amusement and shook his head slightly. 'My God, woman, will you take me there some time?'

'Take you where?'

'To the world you live in. It certainly isn't Planet Earth.'

'Thank you very much,' Lisa said stiffly, her face burning.

'And that's not meant to be an insult,' he told her,

still grinning. 'I do wonder how you ever manage to stand on your own two feet, though.'

Had he, she thought, remembered every word she had told him all those months ago?

'I'll meet you at the yacht,' she said, ignoring the grin which was now getting on her nerves as much as his fatherly, soothing manner had earlier on.

'Fine.' He gave her directions, told her how to get there, asked her again whether she wouldn't be happier if he came to collect her, so that she wondered whether he thought that she would abscond the minute his back was turned for too long, and then gave her a reassuring smile before strolling out of the cottage.

She sat heavily on the bed and contemplated the suitcase on the ground. Why had she come here? What had possessed her? She had wanted to put to rest, once and for all, the gnawing suspicion she had always had that she was dull, unexciting, too willing to settle for the safe path in life. Her parents, her vibrant, roaming parents who'd somehow landed themselves with a daughter who had never shared their wanderlust, would have smiled at her decision. Was that why she had done it? Yes, she thought wearily, of course it was. Except that a few vital things hadn't been taken into the equation.

Now she was here, the guest of a man whose ability to reduce her to a nervous, self-conscious wreck she had forgotten, a man who felt sorry for her, who saw her, even though he had not said so in so many words, as someone who needed a little excitement, someone whose eyes needed opening. From the fast lane in which he had been travelling, he had seen her standing on the lay-by and had reached out and yanked her towards him.

It was a gesture her parents would have appreciated, but, sitting here, she realised that the fast lane was not for her. Yes, he had been right; she was afraid. It was something which he could never in a million years understand because she sensed that fear of the unknown was not something that ever guided his actions. He was one of those people who saw the unknown as a challenge.

Whereas for her, she thought, running a shower and letting the water race over her skin, the unknown was always equated with anxiousness. The anxiousness of leaving one school for another, of meeting new people, of tentatively forging new bonds only for the whole process to be repeated all over again. And every time it had seemed worse.

How could an accident of fate have thrown her into a situation like this?

The following morning, after she had had her breakfast, which, as he had advised her, had been brought to her in her room, she removed herself in her modest black bikini to the beach, selected a deserted patch and lay in the sun, covered with oil.

She would just have to make the best of things. She had decided that as soon as she had opened her eyes and seen the brilliant blue skies outside.

It was impossible to have too many black thoughts when everything around you was visually so beautiful. The sea was crystal-clear and very calm, the sand was white and dusty and there was a peaceful noiselessness about it all that made you wonder whether the hurried life back in England really existed.

She stretched out on her towel, closed her eyes, and was beginning to drift pleasurably off, safe in the knowledge that she wasn't due to meet the yacht for another four hours, when she heard Angus say drily, 'I thought

I'd find you here. You'll have to be careful, though; the sun out here is a killer, especially for someone as fair-skinned as you are.'

Lisa sat up as though an electric charge had suddenly shot through her body and met his eyes glinting down at her seemingly from a very great height.

He was half-naked, wearing only his bathing trunks, and a towel was slung over his shoulder.

Reddening, she looked away from the powerfully built, bronzed torso and said in as normal a voice as she could muster, 'I know. I've slapped lots of suncream on.'

'Very sensible.'

He stretched out the towel and lowered himself onto it, then turned on his side so that he was looking at her.

'What are you doing here?' she asked, keeping her face averted and her eyes closed behind her sunglasses. He was so close to her that she could feel his breath warm on her cheek when he spoke. It was as heady as breathing in a lungful of incense and she hated the sensation.

'I came to your room and you weren't there. I assumed that you'd be out here. Beautiful, isn't it?' He reached out and removed her sunglasses. 'There. That's better. I like to see people when I'm talking to them.'

'May I have my sunglasses back?'

She looked at him and found that he was grinning at her.

'Don't put them on.'

'Is that an order?' she asked primly, and he laughed.

'Would you obey me if it was?'

'No.'

'I didn't think so,' he commented lazily. 'Which is why I'll hang onto them for the moment, if you don't mind.'

She glared at him and he laughed again, this time a little louder.

'What a range of expressions you have,' he said, with the laughter still in his voice. 'From nervousness to fear, to stubbornness, to anger. How old are you?'

She debated informing him that it was none of his business, reluctantly reminded herself that he was her host and was owed some show of good manners, even if he constantly managed to antagonize her, and said coolly, 'Twenty-four.'

'Caroline is nineteen but she seems decades older than you.'

'I'm sorry, I have no idea who you're talking about.' And frankly, her voice implied, I'm not in the least interested, believe it or not.

'The distant cousin.'

Lisa didn't say anything, but her heart sank. The picture in her head was beginning to take shape. The powerful client with his pretentious wife and their precocious child, Caroline, with her well-bred sophistication, Angus, and herself.

'Why are you here?' she asked politely. 'Don't you need to see to your boat? Make sure that all the sails or ropes or whatever are all in the right place?'

'I do hope that there's no implied snub in that question?' he queried with lazy amusement.

'Nothing could be further from my mind.'

'What a relief.' His voice was exaggeratedly serious and she wondered whether the real reason he made her so nervous was that she loathed him. Intensely.

'Actually,' he said, sitting up with his legs crossed and staring down at her, 'I wanted to find you to make sure that you were all right.'

'Why shouldn't I be?' Lying flat on the towel with

only her bikini for protection against those gleaming, brilliant eyes made her feel so vulnerable that she sat up as well and drew her knees up, clasping her arms around them.

'You seemed shaken by the prospect of enforced captivity with the man-eating cannibals I've invited along as guests on this trip.'

'Very funny.'

'No, not terribly,' he said, very seriously now. 'I wanted to find you so that I could reassure you that they're all very nice, perfectly likeable people before you had to confront them.'

'Thank you,' she replied awkwardly. She kept her eyes firmly fixed on his face, stupidly aware of his animal sex appeal. 'I'm sorry I was so garbled last night; it's just that I was taken aback.'

'I realised,' he said drily. 'And I wish you'd stop apologising.'

'Sorry,' she said automatically, and then she smiled shyly, dipping her eyes and gazing out towards the horizon, where the sharp blue line of the sea met the clear blue sky. It was easy to understand why some people believed that to venture beyond that thin blue strip would be to fall off the edge of the earth.

'Did you tell your boss that you were coming on this holiday?' he asked idly, and she could tell that he was staring at her even though she wasn't looking at him. She couldn't tell, though, what he was thinking. Could anyone do that?

'Not exactly,' Lisa admitted. 'I told him that I needed to have a break, that I was tired. Well,' she continued defensively, 'it was more or less the truth.'

'Rather less than more,' he said blandly. 'Did you think that he wouldn't understand?'

'Something like that.' He would have fallen down in shock, she thought with amusement. He knew how much she liked the safe regularity of her job, of her life; she had told him as much when he had first interviewed her years ago for the position.

'I don't want to take on someone who's going to stick around for six months, get bored, and look for more glamorous horizons,' he had said. ·

'Not me,' Lisa had replied. 'There will be no urge to hurry away from this job to look for another one. I have my flat, my roots are here and my job will be for as long as you want me.'

Over the years he had come to know her well enough to realise that her most prized possession was her security. She had bought her small flat with the money which had been left to her on her parents' death, from insurance policies which had secured her future, and there she had been happy to stay, content in her cocoon.

'Because you're not given to taking risks?' Angus prompted now, casually, and she threw him a sharp glance before returning her gaze to the infinitely safer horizon.

'I guess,' she said in a guarded voice.

'Have I invaded personal territory here?' His tone was still light and casual, but she knew that he was probing. Probing to find out about her. It was probably second nature to him, and in her case his curiosity was most likely genuine, the curiosity of someone whose life was so far removed from her own that it really was as though she came from another planet.

'Why are you so secretive?' he asked. He reached out and tilted her face towards his and the brief brush of his fingers on her chin was like the sensation of sudden heat against ice. It was a feeling that was so unexpected that she wiped his touch away with the back of her hand.

'I'm not.'

'You should try listening to yourself some time,' he remarked wryly. 'You might change your mind.'

He stood up abruptly, shook the sand out of his towel and slung it back over his shoulder. Mission accomplished, she thought, except there was a vaguely unsettling taste in her mouth, the taste of something begun and not quite finished.

'Sure you know how to get to the yacht?' he asked, and she nodded.

'So, I shall see you around twelve thirty.'

'Yes,' she murmured obediently, collecting a handful of sand in the palm of her hand and then watching it trail through her fingers.

'And you won't take flight in the interim?' He raised one eyebrow questioningly and then nodded to himself, as though she had answered his question without having spoken. 'No, of course you won't, because, whatever you say, you're as curious now as you are reluctant, aren't you, Lisa?' He stared right down at her and she felt his eyes blazing a way to the core of her. 'This is a new experience for you. You won't regret it. Trust me.'

Then he was gone. She watched him walking slowly away, his lithe body unhurried, and she thought, Are you so sure? Because I'm not.

CHAPTER THREE

WOULD she have been different if she had led a normal kind of life? It was a question Lisa had asked herself over the years and she had never come up with a satisfactory answer.

She was very self-contained, she knew that, just as she knew that most people found her aloof and far too composed for the sort of superficial small talk that made the world go round. Very few had glimpsed the lack of self-confidence behind the composure.

Looking back now, she was old enough and mature enough to realise that this was the real disservice which her parents had unwittingly done her. They had given her variety but her only point of stability had been them, when in fact, at the age of eight or twelve or fourteen, she had needed much more than that. She had needed the stability of a circle of friends, people with whom she could try out her developing personality, learn to laugh without the ridiculous fear of somehow getting it wrong, discover trust without the limits of time cutting it short before it had had time to take root.

When she found herself thinking like that, she never blamed her parents. She accepted it as a *fait accompli*. She had never lacked love; it had not been their fault that she had not been able to fall in with their never-ending travels from one place to another with the same thrill of possible adventure lurking just around the corner.

Her father, a biologist, had been consumed with a

seemingly never-ending supply of curiosity. Nature, in all its shapes and guises, had fascinated him. He would take on a job as gamekeeper to acres of wilderness simply for the satisfaction of exploring the minutiae of the forest life.

Once, for eighteen months, he had worked on the bleak Scottish coastline and had indulged in a brief fling with marine biology, a love which had lived with him until he had died.

That, she thought now, had been the worst time. She could remember having to catch the bus to school in weather that never seemed to brighten. She could remember the smallness of the class, the suspicion of the other children who had treated her with the unconscious cruelty of long-standing village occupants towards the outsider. It had been hard then keeping her chin up but in the end she had made some friends.

Now she could see that it had done nothing for her social self-confidence.

She walked towards the yacht and she could feel the muscles in her stomach tighten just as they had done all those years ago, every time she had walked through the doors of yet another school building.

Everyone else had arrived. She could glimpse the shapes on the boat, the movement, and she hurried a bit more. Someone must have called out something to Angus, because he appeared from nowhere, half-naked, and came down to the jetty to greet her.

The air of restless vitality that seemed to cling to him swept over her and she licked her lips nervously.

'I hope I'm not late,' she began, and he reached out and took the suitcase from her, smiling with that mixture of dry irony and knowing amusement that made her feel so gauche and awkward because it always seemed to imply that he was somehow, somewhere, laughing at her.

'We have a timetable of sorts,' he drawled, 'but we're under no obligation to stick to it. One of the great advantages of a holiday like this. We would have waited for you.'

He turned towards the yacht and she followed him as he threw polite remarks over his shoulder and she made obliging noises in return.

Her legs were feeling heavy and uncooperative, but she took a deep breath and clambered aboard the yacht behind him, allowing him to help her up but then withdrawing her hand as soon as she was there.

From behind the relative protection of her sunglasses, she saw the small circle of people—his guests.

The whole situation inspired the same churning, sinking feeling she had had as a child when she had had to stand up in class, the newcomer, and introduce herself. She made a show of smiling and was swept along on a tide of introductions.

Liz, Gerry, their nine-year-old daughter Sarah, Caroline. They were relaxed, stretched out on loungers on the deck of the yacht, wearing their swimsuits and sipping drinks.

'Now,' Angus said, in that slightly amused, very assured voice of his, 'I shall show Lisa to her cabin.' He turned to her. 'What would you like to drink? We thought we'd have a few drinks here and some lunch before we leave.'

'Anything,' she said obligingly, still smiling, although her jaw was beginning to ache.

'I shouldn't leave the choice open,' Liz said, laughing. 'My husband will simply see that as an invitation to try out one of his lethal homemade cocktails on you and you'll be staggering around before you're halfway finished.'

Gerry laughed and protested at this, and the smile on Lisa's face became a little less forced.

'In that case, I'll have a glass of fruit juice, if I may.'

'Very wise,' Liz said.

'If a little dull.' Caroline hadn't spoken since the introductions had been made. She had stretched out her hand, seen no need to smile and had promptly returned to what she had been doing as soon as the formalities had been concluded: baking under the sun in a turquoise bikini that left very little to the imagination.

Lisa looked at her cautiously, uncertain how to respond to this.

If she was related to Angus, then it was difficult to see the resemblance. Her hair was white-blonde, her eyebrows dark. The only similarity rested on the fact that they were both staggeringly good-looking.

'Don't confuse her,' Angus said amicably, but with an edge of warning in his voice. 'Go back to your sunbathing.'

She removed her huge sunglasses to reveal two very vivid green eyes and glared at him sulkily.

'I'm sure she doesn't need you to look after her,' she said, narrowing her eyes and shifting the direction of their gaze away from Angus and towards Lisa. 'Do you?' She stared assessingly at Lisa.

'I don't need anyone to look after me,' Lisa said politely, feeling embarrassed. 'I've always found that I'm quite capable of doing that myself.'

'Spoken,' Gerry said approvingly from behind her, 'like a true twentieth-century woman.'

Lisa turned towards him with relief.

'All the more surprising, coming as it does from a true eighteenth-century chauvinist,' Liz teased.

They laughed at this shared joke and from behind her adventure book Sarah, without raising her eyes, grinned in the same way an adult would have grinned at the immaturity of two children.

'Now, my dear, what kind of juice would you like?' Gerry, a slightly overweight man in his forties, got up and patted his stomach absent-mindedly.

'Is there a choice?' Lisa asked, surprised.

'Orange, grapefruit, naturally, but also watermelon, mango, pineapple and portugal.'

'The portugal is wonderful,' Liz said helpfully.

'Is it? I'll try that, then. Thank you. I've never had it before.'

'Shall I take her away now?' Angus said from behind her, his voice dry. 'Or is the juice discussion due to continue?'

'Don't be so sarcastic, Angus,' Liz told him, which made him laugh, and Lisa felt his hand on her arm as he escorted her away from the deck and towards her cabin.

The yacht was huge. Immense. And expensively furnished. Lisa looked around her with open curiosity.

'Does it belong to you?' she asked him as he paused in front of a door and pushed it open.

'Yes.' He looked at her. 'Do you like it?'

'Oh, yes, it's wonderful,' she breathed. 'Like a house! I never knew that boats could be as big as this. Not private ones, at any rate.' She flushed, and looked at him. 'You think I'm odd, don't you?' she said with a little laugh, edging round the door and into the room, a difficult manoeuvre because the doorway was very small, and she felt the brush of his body against hers long enough to make her feel a little breathless.

He didn't seem to notice a thing. He walked in, deposited the luggage on the bed and then leaned against the doorframe.

'You were right, anyway,' she continued hurriedly. 'It's all an eye-opener.'

'Good,' he said, sticking his hands into the pockets of his shorts and continuing to look at her. Indolent, amused.

'I'll unpack now, shall I?' The question was supposed to remind him that he had guests above and that she wanted him to leave, but he didn't.

'Was it as bad as you'd feared?'

She was beginning to hate the way he saw her as vulnerable, but she shrugged, and he mimicked the gesture.

'What does that mean?'

'Liz and Gerry seem very nice people,' she said.

'And Caroline?'

'She doesn't look anything like you,' Lisa said, for want of anything else. She hadn't liked Caroline. She hadn't liked the cool condescension she had heard in that precisely manicured voice and she found such perfect looks slightly unsettling.

'You'll have to excuse her,' Angus said, ignoring the remark. 'Caroline is here as a favour to her parents. They find her a bit of a handful.'

'And they think that you might be able to straighten her out?'

'Nothing quite so optimistic, I assure you. Nor am I in the business of straightening people out. Don't let anything she says upset you, though.'

'Thank you for the advice,' Lisa said, coolly, because

he made her sound as though she was a complete walk-over and for some reason she was sick of having him treat her like a minor. 'I'll bear it in mind.'

'It's not meant to be an insult,' he said, raising his eyebrows, and she reddened.

'Of course it isn't,' she replied quickly. 'And I'm grateful for it. Thank you.'

'Oh, for God's sake.' He ran his fingers through his dark hair and shot her an impatient glance from under his lashes. 'Will you stop being grateful?'

'But I am.'

'Unpack,' he said, and she impulsively went towards him and rested her hand on his arm for a fraction of a second.

'Don't be angry.'

'Then stop acting as though I've done you the most enormous favour in inviting you here. As I recall, you weren't exactly grateful to me when you found out that this was to be a cruise of six people and not six hundred.'

'I know that,' Lisa admitted. 'But whether it was six or six hundred it was still very kind of you to think of me enough to issue the invitation.'

'I was responsible for ruining your original holiday,' he reminded her. 'Have you forgotten?'

'But most people wouldn't have taken the trouble to recompense me in the way that you've done.'

'Most people haven't got the money to do it,' he murmured, looking at her, watching her, she knew, for her reaction.

'What do you want me to say to that?'

She looked at him and looked away, feeling her breathing thicken and hoping that he was as unaware of it as she was aware. Why did she react to him like this?

Was it just an understandable physical response, or was it an intellectual one?

She was sensible, she knew, so why did her body ignite the minute he came close to her, when common sense told her that he was off limits? Off limits in the way that screen stars were off limits? They lived in different worlds and only a fool would try to unite the two.

It wasn't as though he was attracted to her. When he looked at her, there was no sexual appraisal in his eyes. She wasn't his type. She was just another average face. Her features were regular, except for her lips, which were too full as far as she was concerned. Her figure was neat but not extraordinary. Her hair fell in a clean swoop to her shoulders and that, like the rest of her, was unexceptional. Background material. If her head could tell her this, then why couldn't her body act accordingly?

'Is that why you felt nervous about this? Because you imagine my wealth puts you at a disadvantage? Or was it because you're unsure of yourself?'

'I'm not unsure of myself!' Lisa denied. 'You hardly know me. How can you say that?'

Her heart was beating quickly. She wished that she hadn't tried to detain him. She wished that she had just let him leave and got on with her unpacking, as he had commanded.

He didn't say anything, which was as telling as if he had argued the point.

'This is none of your business,' she muttered, folding her arms and looking away. 'You invited me here and I came, but *I* am none of your business.'

'Do you ever open up to anyone?' he asked, with less amusement in his voice and considerably more impatience. 'Or do you hide yourself away and let the rest of the human race get on with it?'

'Please may I unpack now?'

'Once you've answered my question. I'm interested.'

'You're curious.'

He shrugged and continued looking at her, waiting for her to answer.

'I don't like being an object of curiosity,' she said stubbornly. Nor, for that matter, do I like being an object of pity, she added to herself. 'It doesn't matter to me how much money you have,' she said, prodded into speech by his silence. 'I've already told you that money makes no difference to what a person's worth. But, of course, here…' She paused and flashed him a quick look from under her lashes. 'Here, I am the odd one out. I don't know the responses I'm supposed to make. I've never had to learn them.'

'How about just being yourself?'

'I thought you didn't like that, because being myself means being secretive and reserved?'

Touché.' He grinned at her with appreciation and she blushed. He straightened his long body. 'Now I'll leave you to unpack. Come up when you're ready and wear a swimsuit.'

'I was going to.'

'Not,' he amended, back to his dry amusement, 'that I want you to think I'm trying to give you orders. I don't want you to see me as a dictator.'

Then how would you like me to see you? she asked herself once he had sauntered off. As a benefactor? As a man? She unpacked quickly, not giving much thought to that choice. She didn't want to see him as a man; she didn't want to catch herself thinking too hard about the supple strength of his body or the disarming charm of his conversation.

She emerged a few minutes later to find her juice next

to an empty lounger, inconveniently next to Caroline, and a platter of sandwiches in the middle. They were all eating, making desultory conversation. Liz, who was reading a book, looked up to say something, then returned to the more drowsy pastime of soaking up the sun.

The heat made everyone lazy. It was impossible to be energetic when it was so hot.

Lisa lay back on the lounger with her broad straw hat shielding her face and surreptitiously looked at Angus, who was talking to Gerry in a low murmur, from the looks of it about work because there was a certain amount of animation to their conversation. He was leaning forward slightly, his elbows resting on his knees. She observed the curve of his back and the latent power of his body and had forgotten about Caroline until the other woman said, *sotto voce*, 'You two took rather a long time down there, considering Angus was just supposed to be showing you to your cabin.'

Lisa didn't say anything, but her body tensed and she looked at the fair-haired beauty warily.

'What were you and he up to?' Caroline laughed a little but there was something hostile behind the laughter.

'Up to?' Lisa asked, puzzled. 'Nothing. Why?' Does he get up to things with women the minute he's alone with one for longer than three seconds? she wanted to ask.

Caroline gave an elegant shrug and fixed her expression to one of indifference. 'Just wondered.' She began to apply some more suntan oil with the unhurried thoroughness of someone who knew that her body was worth looking at. 'It's just,' she continued, when Lisa had hoped that the conversation had been terminated, 'that Angus needs protecting.'

That almost made Lisa laugh, but she managed to say, with some incredulity, 'He does? I'm sorry but I hadn't noticed.'

She stretched out with her towel behind her head and her feet crossed at the ankles. Liz and Sarah were chatting in bursts. After a while they got up from their loungers and strolled out of sight and their voices drifted on the breeze, snippets of information which Liz was trying to impart about tropical fish.

'He explained why he invited you here,' Caroline said languidly, in a low voice.

'Did he?'

'Something about George running into you in the Jag at the airport. He felt sorry for you so he asked you here.'

'It was very kind of him,' Lisa said, for want of anything less inflammatory. She had to remind herself that she was a guest and that outbursts of anger were not advisable, but she could feel her fists clenching and she had to take a few deep breaths to steady herself.

'Yes, it was, which is why I wouldn't want you to take advantage of the fact.'

'I wish you'd get to the point,' Lisa said tightly. 'If there *is* a point. I'm not very good at playing games.'

Caroline turned on her side so that she was facing her and propped her sunglasses on her head. The green, feline eyes, when they looked at her, glittered like emeralds.

'The *point* is that Angus is a very desirable catch and I wouldn't like you to get any ideas in that direction.'

The accusation was so bald that for a minute Lisa stared at her speechlessly. Then she said, without any pretense at politeness, 'In that case, let me just set your mind at rest. He's perfectly safe from *me*. I couldn't care less how eligible your cousin is and I find your remarks insulting.'

Caroline's lips thinned and she seemed on the brink of continuing the subject, but with rather more venom now, when Liz and Sarah returned from their stroll around the deck and general conversation took over. The sandwiches were passed around, drinks were topped up, voices grew louder, as did the laughter, and as soon as the anchor was lifted Lisa removed herself from her lounger and went across to where Liz was standing, holding onto the rails of the boat, with the wind blowing her hair back.

Angus and Gerry were sailing it. They were both highly experienced at it; they had learnt together a long time ago. They had known each other for years, Liz told her, even though Gerry was eleven years older than Angus. Her voice was kind as she provided background material which Lisa only partially heard. She was far more absorbed in the spectacle of the ocean slipping past them and in what Caroline had said to her in that cutting, derogatory voice of hers.

The worst thing was that she could see the logic behind the accusations. Angus was, there was no doubt about it, a good catch. It was surprising, really, that he hadn't been netted before, but if what Liz had told her was anything to go by, then he would hardly have had the time to cultivate any sort of family life. Building empires, it appeared, didn't leave much room for a wife and children and winter evenings in front of the fire.

'He's out of the country most of the time,' Liz was confiding, when Angus said from behind them,

'I do hope you're not talking about me. It's very bad

manners, you know, to discuss your host behind his back.'

Liz laughed and turned to him. 'You should be flattered. I've only said good things about you!'

'Is that true?' Angus turned to Lisa with a slow smile. She felt her heart begin to thud and remembered what Caroline had said.

'Yes, it is,' she said lightly, smiling back at him but finding herself quite unable to meet his eyes straight on. 'She says that you're a very hard worker and that you travel a lot.'

'You make me sound like an ant.' He laughed, turning to Liz. There was a warm empathy between the two of them and Lisa felt a brief pang of envy. Her experience of men was limited and she had certainly never had an easy rapport with any of them. On the whole, she was tense in their company, only relaxing slowly, certainly unable to joke in the semi-flirtatious manner that Liz did.

'I think,' Liz said over her shoulder as she sauntered off to be with Gerry, 'I can spot a few basic differences!'

'She's great fun, isn't she?' Lisa said, looking at him.

'We go back a long way.'

'I envy that,' she heard herself say wistfully, and she abruptly turned away so that she was leaning over the rail, staring down at the sea. She hadn't meant to confide in him. It had just emerged, without prior thought, and now she felt a little awkward.

'The fact that she goes back a long way with me?' Angus asked, laughing.

'No, that wasn't what I meant...'

'I know what you meant.' He leaned over the rail alongside her, their arms almost touching.

'How long before we reach land?' she asked, and he

laughed again, as though he had read her mind and knew that she was trying to change the subject.

'Not very long.'

'Do you do this every year?'

'Social *savoir-faire* isn't something you're born with. It's something that's cultivated. As you said, you just never had to learn the art. I don't suppose there's a great deal of it needed if you work in a garden centre.'

'My father worked in Scotland for a while, but the sea was nothing like this.'

'No, I don't imagine it was. What did he do?'

'He was a biologist.'

'And your mother?'

'A biologist's wife.'

'And you were the biologist's child.'

'That's right. There's something very fierce about the sea in Scotland, even when it's calm.'

He shrugged and she could feel his eyes on her. 'The water here is very blue, very inviting, but you'd be stupid to imagine that it doesn't conceal its own dangers.'

'I heard Liz telling Sarah all about it.'

'I'm surprised you weren't sent to a boarding school.'

'I know a bit about tropical fish, from when my father was going through his marine biology phase. He had books on the subject. You think that I had an unhappy life, but I didn't and I would have hated boarding school.'

'Did your interest in plants come from your father?'

'I suppose so. I've never really thought about it. Why are you asking me all these questions? I don't ask you any.'

'Feel free to.' His lazy charm swept over her and she had to steady herself on the rail before she could turn to face him, shielding her eyes from the sun with the palm of her hand.

'I don't want to. I'm not interested.'

She glanced behind him to where Caroline was still basking like a lizard in the sun. Was she asleep? It was difficult to tell although the large, dark sunglasses were turned in their direction.

'Where are Liz and Sarah?' she asked.

'Liz is with Gerry and Sarah is below deck somewhere. There are limits set as to how much time she spends in the sun. Why didn't you go to university?'

Lisa sighed. She wished that he would stop prying, trying to discover what made her tick, treating her like a specimen under a microscope.

'If you must know,' she said shortly, 'my parents died and it was all I could do to climb through my A levels. I couldn't even contemplate university. I just needed to get some sanity back into my life and having a house and a job represented that.'

'Understandable,' he murmured.

She replied, in a tart voice, 'Oh, I'm so glad you see it like that. It makes me feel much better.' She swept her hair away from her face and narrowed her eyes against the glare of the sun to look at him. 'And what makes *you* tick?' she asked angrily. 'You're so keen to point out all my little inadequacies. Does anything make *you* feel inadequate?'

'No,' he said lazily, 'I don't think so.'

'How lucky you are, then. Swanning through life in your chauffeur-driven car, flying from one important meeting to another, jet-setting across the globe. I expect there are lines of beautiful women queuing up for you as well? To complete the picture, so to speak?'

Now that she had worked herself up to self-righteous

indignation, she would have been more than prepared to carry on with the conversation until the cows came home, but the yacht began slowing down. Bequia, their first port of call, was approaching, and she hadn't even noticed, with her back to the sea and her mind seething with anger.

Liz emerged, with Sarah in tow, her face wreathed in delighted smiles as she walked unsteadily towards them, and Angus said to her, under his breath, 'Don't think that this conversation is finished.' He wasn't looking at her when he said this, nor was there any amusement etched on his face.

'Is that a threat?' She wouldn't have said it if she had thought about it.

'A promise.' He pushed himself away from the railing and began preparing the yacht for docking.

Caroline didn't move until the yacht was moored; then she lazily stood up, shaking her hair, which obediently fell back into place, and slung a silk shirt over her swimsuit.

She must, Lisa thought, be quite accustomed to this sort of thing, because she didn't look in the least excited—or perhaps excitement was something that she no longer indulged in at the ripe old age of nineteen.

Two nights in Bequia, Liz was telling her. She was to bring next to nothing from the yacht. If she needed anything, she could always go and get it, but really they would just be sunbathing, swimming and indulging in the odd water sport, if energy levels permitted.

Lisa was glad of the advice. She slipped on a pair of shorts and a halter-neck top and managed to stuff everything she wanted into her holdall, so that she didn't emerge from her cabin five minutes later laden down with three times more than she needed.

They took two taxis to the hotel. She travelled in one
with Liz and Sarah, and Angus, Gerry and Caroline took
the other. She spent the short journey chatting to Sarah
about the plant life, just as her father used to do with
her when she was a child. She described what grew
where and why and what harboured which sorts of insects. Facts which she had thought she had forgotten
sprang back to memory and she surprised herself with
the extent of her knowledge.

The taxis disgorged them outside the hotel, a secluded
plantation estate, set in rambling orchards of tropical
fruit trees.

She looked around her and couldn't imagine that anything, anywhere in the world, could surpass this ageless,
discreet magnificence. It was the unspoken epitome of
what money could buy. Liz and Gerry had been before,
and were pointing out things that had changed, and
Caroline, after a quick glance around, stretched grace-
fully and announced that she was off to the pool.

'Too much sun is bad for you,' Sarah said, holding
her mother's hand, and Caroline scowled.

'Bad for *you* maybe, but not me. Oh, no, I intend to
return to England with something to show for two weeks
in the Tropics!'

'You already have a marvellous tan,' Liz said, and
Caroline nodded smugly in agreement, then vanished towards her room.

'And what about you?' Angus turned to Lisa, and she
smiled politely.

'I think I shall go to the beach. Why don't you come
with me, Sarah?' She looked away from those piercing
blue eyes to the little girl.

'Only for half an hour,' Liz warned, and they both
nodded.

'Worries too much, I think,' Sarah said as they strolled along the beach, collecting shells.

'Of course she does! She's your mother. Mine used to worry about insect bites and poisonous plants.'

When she delivered Sarah back to the hotel, she found herself, much to her disgust, peering in the direction of the pool to see whether Angus was there. I don't care where he is, she told herself, but if he's by the pool then I shan't feel as though I've got to be on the lookout.

He wasn't there. Then she hated herself for wondering where he was.

She wished that she could block him out of her mind totally; she wished that she could look at him without feeling nervous; she wished that she could converse with him in a natural manner and then relegate everything he said to some compartment at the back of her mind. Somewhere safe and unthreatening.

She set off for the beach, which was virtually isolated, and lay down on her towel with her eyes closed.

When she next opened them, she was staring at the deep blue cloudless sky. She thought that if a painter ever decided to capture this on canvas the painting would be awful. The lines too defined, the colours too vivid and surreal, everything shimmering with an intensity that defied belief.

With a small sigh of contentment, she headed out to the water, which was nearly as warm as bath water, and struck out, swimming far and fast, leaving the beach behind, then turning round and treading water and looking back at the island from her vantage point.

The view was breathtaking. White sand, like powder, clear water lapping lazily up to the shore and falling back. The sound of the breeze and the sea was like a whisper, rising and sinking and never-ending.

She swam back in, slower, lazier, and surfaced to see Angus standing by her beach towel, his arms folded and a scowl on his face.

'What the hell do you think you're doing?' He waited until she was close before saying anything, and his voice was low and sharp.

'Wh-what? What do you mean?' Lisa stammered in confusion. She bent down to scoop up her towel and he pulled it away from her and flung it on the sand.

'Answer me!'

'Swimming!' she said hurriedly, backing away. 'What's the matter? Is something wrong?' She was beginning to feel a little lost. Why was he so angry? Had something happened? Had she done something wrong without realizing it?

'Look around you. What do you see?'

Lisa looked around her and then back at him. 'I don't see anything.'

'Precisely. The beach is empty, isn't it?'

'Yes.' What was he trying to say to her? 'It must be later than I thought. What time is it? I left my watch back at the hotel when I came out here.'

'The time is immaterial. What I want to know is what the hell you think you're doing, swimming when there's no one around.'

'Oh.' She nearly smiled in sheer relief. 'The water is quite safe,' she continued, noticing that his expression was still as black as thunder.

'And what if you had got yourself into trouble out there?'

'Well, I didn't.' She was beginning to feel resentful. 'I'm a strong swimmer.' The sun had left the sky. Twilight was creeping up.

'What kind of answer is that?'

'Look,' she said in a placating voice, 'I'm sorry you were worried, or concerned, or whatever, but I was quite safe.' She took a deep breath and said what she felt ought to be said, because she was tired of being treated like a child. 'My welfare isn't your concern. I'm a big girl now and I can take care of myself.' She sat down on her towel, painstakingly spreading it out so that it was flat, and hoped that he would go away and leave her alone.

To her dismay, he sat down next to her and now she began to feel conscious of her swimsuit.

'Oh, you are, are you?' he said tautly.

'That's right. I am. Now perhaps we should head back in.' She started to get up and he reached out, hardly shifting his position at all, and circled her wrist with his fingers.

'What do you think you're doing?'

'I'm not ready for you to go,' he said, unperturbed. 'You tell me that you're a big girl, that you can look after yourself. Well, Lisa, why don't you prove it?'

CHAPTER FOUR

'PROVE it?' Lisa said. The shadows were gathering around them. The angular lines of his face had softened, but his expression was unreadable, although she could still see the glitter in his eyes and the faint curve of his mouth.

'That's right.' He still hadn't let go of her hand and the warm pressure of his fingers on her skin was sending her into a state of muted panic. She wasn't sure what he wanted from her; her mind just couldn't seem to work its way round what his words had implied.

'I don't know what you mean; I don't know what you're talking about. Please,' she said in a half-whisper. 'I'm really not accustomed to…this…'

'To what?' His voice sounded faintly surprised, but she knew that he wasn't. He had left his hand where it was because he knew that it threw her into a lather and he was enjoying the spectacle of that, like a cat playing with a mouse, not necessarily with a view to a kill, but certainly with a view to having a bit of fun.

'I think we ought to go back inside…'

'Why? I'm your host. Can't you relax enough to have a conversation with me?'

She laughed nervously, but she could feel her heart beating rapidly and the blood rushing round her body, making her hot and tense. She'd had few men in her life, no serious relationships, never a kiss that made her freeze or a hand that inflamed—nothing, nothing that could have prepared her for the surge of sheer yearning that swept through her and left her feeling as though she had been hurled blindly in every direction by a tidal wave.

The vehemence of the emotion left her winded but suddenly strong enough to speak.

'Of course I can, if that's what you want. It's just that I'm beginning to feel a little cold and uncomfortable out here.'

'Cold?' He shot her a disbelieving look. 'I can't possibly understand that. It's still pretty hot out here, and besides...' he paused and allowed his eyes to wander along her body before returning to her face '...your swimsuit covers you up so thoroughly that I doubt you can be feeling even remotely cold.'

It was the first time that he had assessed her physically, and she wondered whether she had imagined it. Had she? She convinced herself nervously that she had, and tried to hang onto her composure.

'You and Caroline seemed to be having a very cosy conversation on the yacht earlier on,' he said lazily. She felt him stroke the soft flesh of her inner wrist, a gesture which to her confused mind seemed shockingly intimate.

'Were we?'

'What was she telling you?'

'I can't remember.' Lisa lowered her eyes. Her body felt as though it was being kept in a state of unnatural stillness; one false move and it would fall apart.

'Of course you can,' he said mildly. 'Tell me.'

'I'd rather not. I'd rather we went back to the hotel. I'd rather you let go of my hand.'

'And I'd rather do neither of those things. So it would appear that we're at a stalemate, wouldn't it? I don't like stalemates.'

The silence thickened around them, and eventually

she said, reluctantly, 'She's concerned about you. If you really want to know, she thinks you need protecting.'

'Does she? Protecting from what? Or should I say...from whom?'

'From me,' Lisa said huskily. She couldn't look at him when she said this and she resented the fact that the information had been torn out of her.

He let go of her hand and looked at her thoughtfully. 'I think that perhaps Caroline and I should have a little talk. Cousin to cousin.'

'No! Please don't.' Lisa looked at him miserably. 'I wouldn't want to land anyone in trouble and anyway, she had your interests in mind. I would probably have done the same thing if I had been in her position.'

'I don't imagine that you would,' Angus said flatly. 'The problem with Caroline is that she can't resist men. She flits from one relationship to another and she assumes that every other woman is motivated in the same way that she is. She's on this cruise recovering from a broken engagement. The third she's called off in the space of under two years.'

'Please don't say anything...'

'You say that you would have done the same thing if you were in her position, but you're nothing like her, are you?'

'No,' Lisa mumbled. Incoherence was beginning to set in. Her mouth felt dry, and she could hardly get the words out without a great deal of effort. 'She's very beautiful.'

'I'm not talking about looks,' he said impatiently. 'Do you flit from one man to another?'

'I suppose not.'

'Have you ever had a lover?'

She could feel his eyes on her, staring at her intently, and the darkness gave them a brooding look.

'That's none of your business.' The thought of her virginity sent a flood of shame coursing through her, making her face burn. What right did he have to ask these questions? What right did he have to assume that he could ferret information out of her simply because he happened to be her host?

'Have you?'

She hesitated for a fraction of a second and knew that the silence had spoken the words she couldn't bring her mouth to formulate.

'I've been meaning to,' she said defensively. 'I take relationships seriously. I've never found anyone... Of course, I've had boyfriends!'

'Naturally.'

She sprang up and began walking away. Her eyes were hurting from tears which she refused to shed, tears of embarrassment and mortification.

'There's more to being an adult than having sexual experience!' she shouted at him, stopping to turn around and surprised to find him on her heels.

'Of course there is.'

'And stop agreeing with me! Do you think I don't realise you're being patronizing? I'm not a fool!'

'No. You're not.'

'There you go again.'

'Would you prefer me to argue with you?'

'It might make a pleasant change! It might make me feel more of a person and less of a charity case!'

He shook his head and then held her by her shoulders and said, enunciating very carefully, 'Stop telling me how sorry I feel for you. How can there be room to feel sorry for you when you're so busy feeling sorry for yourself?'

'That's not true.'

He gave her a little shake, as though it was the only way to make her listen to him, but she was listening, listening with every pore in her body, listening to sounds in her mind and the silences between what he was saying.

'You can't put your past behind you,' he told her. 'It follows you around like an albatross tied to your neck. You came here on a crazy impulse, but now that you're here you can't shed your inhibitions, can you?'

'Why are we talking about this? What has this got to do with anything? I don't want you analysing me.'

'Because you're afraid that I might be more truthful than you'd like?'

'Because it's none of your business—I keep telling you.'

'And I'm telling you that it is.'

They stared at each other and the stillness of the night was like a weight pressing down on her, turning her to fire.

'Why do you think that you're not beautiful?' he asked huskily. His hand moved to the curve of her neck. 'You make a point of saying that money doesn't determine a person's worth. Do you think that appearance does?'

She didn't know what to say. His voice had changed; it was thicker, less controlled, and he was breathing quickly—as quickly as she was. She could see the rise and fall of his chest and she watched, fascinated, unable to move, unable to speak.

His fingers coiled into her hair and he pulled her towards him, bending down slightly so that the features of his face became indistinct. She closed her eyes and thought that she should run away, as fast as she could, but her muscles felt sluggish, and besides, she wanted what was going to happen. She wanted him to kiss her.

Their lips met and she groaned with what was either denial or desire—maybe both. She could feel his hard body pressed against her and his hand moved to mould the small of her back.

His lips, at first gentle and persuasive, moved with a hunger now that sent a shudder through her. His tongue found hers, exploring deeper and harder, and her breasts, pushing against his chest, ached to be touched.

This was the naked face of passion—something she had only ever read about in books. She had never realised the real depth of her innocence until now, when desperate yearning reached out from inside her and spiralled through every vein in her body. It frightened her but at the same time she couldn't stop herself.

Her head fell back as his tongue trailed a burning path along her neck. He was breathing thickly and unevenly and she whimpered as he peeled the shoulder straps of her swimsuit from her shoulders and pulled them down to her waist so that her small breasts were exposed.

She didn't try to pull away. She whimpered in shock and pleasure as his hand cupped one breast, caressing it, while his thumb rotated against the nipple until it hardened to his touch.

She had small breasts but her nipples were large and sensitive and seemed to throb under the impact of his fingers. Her body was trembling, reduced to nothing more than a receptacle for sensations never experienced before.

He bent to take one nipple into his mouth, sucking hard on it while his hands worked her swimsuit still lower. In the process, wrapped around each other, they sank to the sand. Did he let her go for an instant? He must have because now there was a towel beneath her and she had no idea how it had got there. She was so consumed by his lovemaking that she really thought nothing could break through the flaming haze around them, not rain or thunder or even an army of soldiers on the beach.

His fingers played with her breasts as he kissed the bare column of her neck, caressing them, teasing them, squeezing them. She had to feel the wetness of his mouth and she pushed his head lower so that he could take the throbbing peaks into his mouth.

She was prepared to go the whole way; she thought that the intensity of blinding desire would be enough. It was only when she felt his hand move against her thigh, parting her legs, that her thought processes, which had been frozen into inactivity, churned back into life.

She could see herself now and it was like looking down at herself from a great height. Ordinary little Lisa, in pigtails and with her schoolbooks under her arm, ordinary little Lisa in her first party dress, so nervous that she felt sick, ordinary little Lisa lying on a beach with her natural reserve scattered to the four winds, making love with a man who had succumbed to some bizarre, passing whim.

His hand slipped underneath her swimsuit and she wriggled frantically, with all the energy she could muster, pulling away from him.

It's not enough! she thought.

'What's wrong?' His voice sounded slurred and disoriented and seemed to reach her from a long way away.

'I can't do this!' she whispered hoarsely, and he

pinned her back so that she couldn't do what she wanted most to do, which was to spring to her feet and run away.

'You can't stop now,' he grated savagely, and she looked away from him.

'You're hurting me.'

He let her go and she stayed where she was, shivering, as though it had suddenly turned bitterly cold.

'I'm sorry—' she began, but he cut her short with a snarl.

'Forget it.'

'I didn't mean to…I didn't mean for anything like this to happen…'

'I said, forget it.' He stood up and began walking away and she hurried to keep pace with him.

It hurt with a pain that was almost physical to think of their lovemaking. When was it ever going to end? She had come over here on impulse, she had gone against everything she had instilled into herself, and, as if that wasn't bad enough, she had committed the cardinal sin of being attracted to Angus Hamilton.

She had recognized the attraction, but what she had failed to do was acknowledge the power it had over her. Her inexperience had opened doors which should have remained shut. Was that what had turned him on? Her inexperience? The moonlight? A combination of both? It certainly hadn't been a meeting of minds, because in the naked glare of reason it was easy to see that a meeting of minds for them was out of the question.

She glanced across at the dark figure striding back towards the plantation and felt another wave of horror wash over her.

'You're angry, I know,' she said timidly, and was relieved when he didn't jump down her throat, although he hadn't slowed down and didn't appear to be listening to a word she said. 'It's just that I'm not the type of person who...'

'There's no need for a lengthy post-mortem, Lisa,' he said coldly, not looking at her.

'I'm not giving you a lengthy post-mortem, I just want to explain...'

'So that you can feel better about what we did?'

'No.' That's exactly why, she thought miserably. She wanted to explain things so that she could put the incident behind her and justify her behaviour to herself. She wished that he would slow down.

He must have read her mind because he stopped abruptly and looked down at her, his face hard.

'Then do explain why, if it makes you feel better. I'm all ears.'

'Something happened—I don't know what...'

'I think it's called sexual attraction.'

'Whatever.' She couldn't say it; she couldn't allow herself to admit that something as untamed as sexual attraction had turned everything she believed in on its head.

'No, not *whatever*. Sexual attraction. Say it!'

'All right! Sexual attraction. Is that better?' She looked at him defiantly. 'I was caught up in the moment and I'm sorry but I let myself...do something that I would never have done if I'd been thinking straight.'

'How terrible,' he snarled. 'The end of the world.'

'Not the end of the world, no!' she said angrily, hating him for the power he had over her and hating herself for her weakness. 'But a mistake. I just want to say that I made a mistake and if I led you on then I apologise.'

'Apology accepted,' he said tersely. He began walking off again and she had to half run to keep up with the pace of his long legs.

Of course he was still angry. Why shouldn't he be? As far as he was concerned, she had sent out signals only to retreat hurriedly when the moment of decision had come. Women, she thought resentfully, didn't play those sorts of games with him. For him, the step from mutual attraction to lovemaking was a simple one. There were no questions about love, or the rightness or wrongness of what they were doing.

'It won't happen again,' she told him. The hotel lights were up ahead, and with every step closer to civilisation her feeling of stupidity over what she had nearly done grew.

'No, I'm sure it won't.'

She took a deep breath. 'The fact is that you're just not my type.'

He paused outside the hotel and looked down at her. His face was coldly curious.

'And who is? What is your type?'

'I don't know...,' Lisa whispered uncomfortably. Not you, she thought. Not someone as good-looking, as clever, as wealthy, as unassailable as you, that's for sure. Not someone who will dally with average little me because the opportunity is there, and then move on to more glamorous types the minute the opportunity arises.

How many women with more convincing credentials had tried to get him to put a ring on their finger? she wondered. Self-confident women with coy smiles and loud voices and perfect faces...

'Come on,' he said, with a humourless, assessing smile. 'Surely you can do better than that?'

She didn't say anything.

'Shall I help you out?' he asked politely. 'You don't jump into the sack with a man simply because you're attracted to him. Oh, no, that would be too easy. What you want is a man who is going to guarantee undying love, and maybe then, if he fulfils the rest of the ridiculous criteria you've laid down in that head of yours, you might consider doing something spontaneous.'

'That's not fair!'

'Except,' he continued, ignoring her outburst, 'there are no guarantees in life.'

'I know that! I don't expect guarantees! You just can't accept the fact that you've been turned down by a woman. I bet it's something that's never happened to you in your life before!'

She could feel the colour burning in her cheeks. 'You've always been able to take what you wanted, and you thought that you would be able to take me as well. You're angry because your pride has been hurt, and you're trying to blame me for it, trying to insinuate that the reason I won't sleep with you, the reason I couldn't, is because of my inadequacies. The simple truth is that I was swept away because, yes, I *am* inexperienced, and, yes, you *are* an attractive man—but I just didn't find you attractive *enough*.'

His eyes narrowed. Had she said too much? Every word had been more or less the truth, but, considering she had been trying to pour oil on troubled waters, she hadn't made a wild success of it, had she? He looked as though he wanted to kill her.

'I'm sorry,' she muttered. 'I shouldn't have said that.'

'Why not? It's always a good idea to clear the air.' He threw her another freezingly polite smile. 'Points us in the right direction, makes sure that things are black and white, with no awkward grey bits in between.'

'Yes,' she said uncertainly. She met his stare briefly and licked her lips.

'So now we can carry on as though nothing has happened.'

'Yes.' She nodded with relief. That, she thought, would be best. To pretend nothing had happened. That way she might be able to shove the memory of his hands on her body, the memory of the way she had felt, into the background, and get on with things in the only way she knew how.

He turned on his heel and stalked off, and after a while she headed back to her room and sank down on the bed with a sigh.

She shut her eyes and saw them together on the beach, her heart racing, her body straining for his. She would never have believed she was capable of anything like that. When she'd been growing up, her life had been controlled to a large extent by her parents, by their constant travelling. When they had died, she had taken control for the first time. She had bought her flat, she had found her job, she had made sure that everything in her life fell into place the way she wanted it to.

She had never really sat down and thought about what sort of man she would end up with, but she had known he would be as unthreatening to her as every other aspect of her life.

She dressed slowly for dinner, and she wondered anxiously whether she would be able to look at him without flinching, without her face telling the world what had happened. She wondered whether her voice would sound normal when she spoke.

But when she joined the others in the dining room, and glanced warily at him as she sat down, their eyes met for the briefest of moments across the table and she realised with relief and a strange sort of disappointment that it would all be easy. Nothing happened, those remarkable blue eyes said icily. You can go back to your hiding hole.

This is life, she told herself, and it is what you wanted. Remember?

Still, it was a shame. She would never have this chance again, this opportunity to see places so beautiful that paradise became reality instead of just a word conjured up on the back of a holiday brochure.

Mustique, which prosaically took its name from the French word for mosquito but had none, small enough to walk around inside a few hours, exclusive to the point of absurdity, flowed into Canouan, with its hidden coves and beaches, which flowed into Mayreau. Then the Tobago Cays, with water so clear that you could see every grain of sand underneath. Lisa snorkelled there, for the first time in her life, and saw underwater scenes that were unimaginable unless seen at first hand.

She saw more islands—beautiful little emerald and sapphire blobs in the middle of the ocean, picture postcards for her to remember from photographs and memories in the years to come.

But as the yacht sailed down the glorious Grenadines everything was so overshadowed by Angus's presence that it all seemed to slip past in a blur.

Not that things didn't carry on as normal, on the surface, because they did. She smiled and laughed and chatted and grew browner under the sun and pretended that Angus's remoteness wasn't affecting her. She watched him from under her lashes and saw everything even when her attention was apparently somewhere else. It was as though her whole body was sensitised to such a degree that everything he said or did, every nuance of every action, was filed away in her mind.

With only a couple of days of the holiday left, she found herself yearning to return to the refreshing normality of her life with its pleasant routines.

Angus intended to dock the yacht off Grenada and they would spend their final night there before flying back to London.

They had breakfast aboard the yacht the following morning, which was lovely. Lisa relaxed on her chair and stared out at the horizon and at the turquoise water. The sun, even at that hour, was already hot. She was as brown as Caroline now and the colour suited her. Her face, she knew, seemed more vibrant, the chocolate-brown of her eyes less uninspiring. She had the sort of colouring which, when its usual pale shade, did not stand out, but which, when tanned, made her look exotic. She half closed her eyes and let the conversation drift around her.

'Super little market...fresh fruit...'

'Must get some souvenirs for the girls at the bridge club...'

'Grand Anse beach is lovely; do you remember it? Shall we meet for lunch at the hotel there? Have a swim...?'

'Darling, have I put on a ghastly amount of weight? Be honest.,,'

The voices floated over her head. They were making plans but she was too pleasantly lulled by the sun to make any contribution. The sun made everyone too lazy to discuss anything with much vigour, even the planning of the day—their last day.

It was only when she heard Angus mention her name that her mind refocused and she sat up abruptly to find him looking at her.

'I'm sorry,' she said, flustered. 'I missed that.'

Liz made some remark about the sun and its soporific effect, to which Gerry illogically replied that if his financial director hadn't sorted out that tax business for the accountants his head would be on the block, and Lisa repeated, 'What were you saying?' She didn't think that he had addressed her at all for days on end, not directly.

'Caroline is going to spend the day on the beach,' he said casually, and there was an odd look in his eyes, as though he was being very careful not to reveal too much. 'Since it's our last day here and you've never been this way before, I've decided to take you on a tour of the island. You'll be fascinated by the plant life over here.'

'Thank you, but really, I'd rather just laze around.' You've decided? she thought. And so I must fall in? Like the last time?

'I'm sure Lisa would much rather do her own thing than trek around the island with you in this heat.' Caroline's voice, which seemed disembodied because her eyes were hidden, as usual, behind her sunglasses, was sharp.

'I'm sure Lisa is quite capable of making up her own mind, Caroline,' Angus drawled, his eyes on Lisa's face. 'You can't leave the island without seeing the plant life,' he told her blandly. 'Unless, of course, you have other, personal reasons for not coming with me?'

'No, of course not,' she said brightly, with a laugh. There had been a soft challenge in his voice and now he smiled the smile of the victor, knowing that he had trapped her.

'Good. Then that's settled.' And he relaxed back with his hands clasped behind his head, while Liz resumed the conversation, asking interested questions about her job at the garden centre, and Caroline sat stiffly back with a frown on her face.

'My mother is interested in plants as well,' she said, dipping into the conversation and silencing everyone in the process. 'Does a lot for the Chelsea Garden Show. Has a permanent stall there every year. Such a bore. I like flowers but I simply don't see the point of labouring over them, not when you can pay someone else to do it.'

'You don't see the point of labouring over anything, Caroline,' Angus pointed out, looking at his watch.

'Why bother when you don't have to?' she asked, and Angus didn't bother to answer.

Caroline's conversations always seemed to take the same course. She stated, everyone listened, and if none of her statements seemed to provoke lively discussion, then it didn't seem to trouble her because she simply returned to whatever it was she had been doing in the first place. Every now and again she had mentioned her ex-fiancé, with an air of boredom, and Lisa got the impression that very little roused her out of her self-centred little universe, in which she always had the starring part.

Very little except Angus, perhaps. Did she have a crush on him? She did look at him quite a bit when she thought that no one was watching, but then so did most women, she had noticed. He had the sort of dark, arresting face that attracted stares.

The yacht docked and amid the general chatting, clutching of hats and impossible arranging of times when they would meet and where Angus stalked off in search of a car to hire.

'What fun for you,' Liz said, beaming, 'driving around the island with Angus, looking at all those wonderful plants and flowers. What a clever idea of his!'

'Very clever, yes,' Lisa said, trying to look enthusiastic.

She watched wistfully as Liz, Gerry and Sarah bustled off, leaving Caroline behind, elegant in silk shorts and a sleeveless shirt and a large straw hat which shaded all of her face.

'Aren't you going with them?' Lisa asked politely.

'I just wanted a few words,' she said, and Lisa sighed.

'Look…' she began, and then stopped and thought, Why am I apologising for this arrangement? It's hardly as though I engineered the thing.

'No, *you* look. Look at yourself. I suppose you think it's started raining money, being invited along with Angus on a trip round the island. I suppose you imagine that your boat's come in…'

'No, of course—'

'You, in your dowdy little department-store outfits! He's out of your reach.'

'You're getting hold of the wrong end of the stick, Caroline…' she began again, on the brink of apologising and then thinking better of it.

'No, I'm not! It's obvious that you have a crush on him and I'm just doing you a favour by telling you to steer clear.'

'Why should you care?' Lisa asked curiously, and Caroline flushed. 'He's out of your reach as well,' she continued gently. 'I'm not interested in him and I'm certainly not some kind of fortune hunter.' She paused and frowned. 'I understand why you feel protective of him, but Caroline, he just sees you as a child; he—'

'Why don't you mind your own business?' Caroline said, white-faced.

'Liz is waving for you to go.' It was a pointless argument. 'You'll get left behind.'

'You're not in our class.'

'Nor would I want to be,' Lisa informed her with a rush of anger.

'Just so long as we understand one another.' She trounced off, her blonde hair whipping back from under the hat as she half ran, her arms folded.

Lisa waited, and after twenty minutes Angus returned with a bunch of keys. For someone who had pushed her into a corner, he didn't seem terribly thrilled at the prospect that lay ahead. His face was grim.

'We needn't go on this trip,' she said nervously, 'if you've changed your mind. I'm very happy to spend the last day on the beach.'

'I'm sure you are,' he replied tersely, angry with her for reasons which she couldn't begin to fathom but which hardly promised an enjoyable and carefree day. 'I'm sure you'd love nothing better than to be in company instead of condemned to enforced isolation with me, but that's just too bad.' He walked off towards an ageing blue car, opened the passenger door for her and then installed himself in the driver's seat.

'Have you brought a map?' she asked, after a while. 'Honestly, Angus,' she said, when he still hadn't started the engine, 'I don't think this is a good idea.'

'It's a damn good idea,' he contradicted her, in a voice that bordered on aggressive. He looked at her and she fell silent. 'I haven't brought a map, in answer to your question. I've decided we'll just take the inland road and see what happens.'

Lisa didn't say anything. She didn't relish the thought of an aimless drive with him, possibly getting lost somewhere along the line, but she also didn't relish the thought of arguing the point with him.

'Cat got your tongue, Lisa?' he asked, driving off at a leisurely pace which she suspected had more to do with the car than with him. 'Or have you been stunned into silence at the adventure that lies ahead?' He gave a dry laugh and she remained silent. She could cope with nerves, but something about him made her uneasy. What lay ahead? She didn't know and she didn't much want to find out.

CHAPTER FIVE

LISA stared out of the window. There was no air-conditioning in the car and even with the breeze sifting through her hair she still felt hot and sticky and vaguely plastered to the seat with perspiration.

He was, she thought, in a foul mood, and she wondered why he had bothered to invite her along in the first place, especially knowing that she hadn't wanted to come, and why, when she had offered to forget about the whole trip, he had ignored the suggestion. And she had no idea how to break the silence between them. She had never been much good at aimlessly chatting about nothing in particular, and besides, the brooding harshness of his face was putting her off.

At least he seemed to know where he was going, though, even without the help of a map. He had been here before. Who knew? Maybe he had driven this same route with another woman, some poor woman who had now been relegated to the past.

She glanced sideways at him, felt that familiar lurching in her stomach, and hurriedly directed her attention back through the car window.

They had left the coast behind now, heading towards the centre of the island, over mountains and along narrow, uneven and very windy roads.

She stopped thinking about him and started paying attention to the scenery unfolding outside. After a diet of sand and sea, she was unprepared for the savage lushness of the landscape around them. It seemed to engulf them from all sides. She forgot that he was in a bad temper and that she was a bag of nerves, and started talking about the immense variety of plants and flowers.

'My father would have loved this,' she said. 'He would have gone quite mad. He would have been out there, hopping around, dissecting leaves and looking for bugs. He used to bring things home, all kinds of insects and plant life, and show them to me and Mum. Do you know, I could draw a diagram of a cross-section of a leaf before I could read?' She laughed, with her head turned away from him. 'I don't suppose that's proved a very useful talent, mind you.' She laughed again and this time she glanced around to look at him.

He wasn't as grim as he had been when they had first started out, but there was still something unreadable about his expression which was unsettling. She reverted to the less intimidating inspection of the trees.

Town life had already disappeared, to be replaced by village life, and now that too was vanishing as wilderness took over. Trees and forest land rearing up on either side of the road were restrained from making a complete take-over by the bumpy strip of tarmac. Occasionally they passed a house or two, primitive, picturesque dwellings precariously balanced on patches of cleared land. Even less occasionally they passed people, and when they did they were stared at with silent curiosity.

She wished, she said, that she had brought some books with her so that she could identify more.

'It's all so tame at a garden centre,' she explained, not wanting to take her eyes off the roadside in case she missed something. 'All neatly laid out in tubs and boxes. Even the exotic plants like the orchids seem strange and lifeless compared to out here where they grow wild. Am

I boring you?' She shot him an anxious glance and he smiled, a real smile, warm and amused.

'Shall I stop so that you can get out and have a closer look at everything?'

'Would you mind very much?'

So she clambered out and had a look around and picked a few flowers growing wild at the side of the road then scrambled back into the car.

'For me?' he asked drily, eyeing the flowers when she was back inside the car, and he smiled again so that she went pink and felt a little flustered.

'I thought they'd match your shirt,' she joked.

'I'll stick one behind my ear, shall I?' he asked.

'I'm glad you're in a better mood.' She couldn't imagine what prompted her into saying that. Relief, maybe, that he wasn't scowling? She felt light-hearted and carefree. If she'd had anything of a voice, she might even have sung.

'Was I in a bad mood? No,' he continued, glancing at her sideways then concentrating on the road again, 'don't answer that.'

'Was it something I did?' She frowned, thinking back.

'Why do you always blame yourself for everything?'

'Habit, I guess,' she answered, surprising herself again. 'I grew up blaming myself for not being like my parents and I suppose I never really stopped.' She laughed self-consciously and turned away.

They had reached the top of the island now. Everything gave way to the Grand Etang, an extinct volcanic crater, a great yawning mouth of flat, metallic blue water that gave you the creepy feeling of immeasurable depth.

They got out of the car to stretch their legs. Away from the crater, they could plunge into the rainforest and

Lisa looked longingly at it, conjuring up the bamboo trees, the creeping vines, the dark silence broken only by the sounds of birds and wild animals.

For a fleeting second, and for the first time, she felt a vivid empathy with her parents and their constant quest for new things. Then she blinked and the feeling was gone.

There was no one else around. No tourists, no locals.

'We are the first people to discover this,' she announced with her arms outstretched. 'Shall we fly our flag and name it after us?' She laughed, delighted, and he grinned at her.

'You're like a child with a new toy,' he said, amused.

'Can you blame me?' She walked towards him and looked up at him seriously. 'I've never seen anything like this in my life before. My parents may have cultivated the art of travelling, but never outside England, and besides, when you're being dragged along, it's difficult after a while to appreciate new things without feeling a little jaundiced. When you're eleven or twelve or thirteen, moving from one place to another is just disorienting, or at least it was for me. There's no excitement, there's just that horrible tearful feeling of saying goodbye to people whose faces you were just beginning to grow accustomed to.'

'Some might have seen all that constant travel as a way of making hundreds of friends.'

'True,' Lisa said, walking back slowly towards the car, 'but not me. I don't think I was ever extrovert enough for that.' She laughed and said brightly, 'Why are we being so serious when the sun is shining and the birds are singing and it's our last day on this wonderful island?'

'Because,' Angus said softly from beside her, 'I want to get through to you.'

Lisa didn't say anything. For the past hour or so he had been her companion; she had relaxed with him, she had laughed with him, she had forgotten her nerves. Now he was a man again and her nerves were back. The silky intent in his voice, the awareness of his blue eyes on her face were like the touch of something warm and inviting and dangerous.

She slipped into the passenger seat, slammed the door and waited, without looking, for him to get in. She expected him to continue his line of thought, and she could already feel the muscles in her stomach tensing in preparation, but he didn't. He flicked on the engine and began driving away from the crater and out towards the coast on the windward side.

When he spoke, it was about normal things, things she could deal with; he asked her questions about work and whether she was looking forward to getting back, about her plans for the future, about her friends, about what she did in the evenings in Reading. Was there much of a night-life? he asked, and laughed when she told him that the only night-life she seriously considered was a cup of hot chocolate in front of the television, with her legs curled up underneath her and her book on her lap. On weekends she saw friends.

'And no boyfriend,' he stated conversationally, and she ignored him, which made him laugh again, although there was a hard edge to his laughter.

They reached Grand Anse, sticky and tired, and Angus turned to her and said in a dry voice, 'There, back in one piece. Was it as much of an ordeal as you'd expected?'

'Thank you,' she said, looking down so that her hair

fell across her eyes and she had to sweep it aside with her hand. 'It was wonderful.'

And that, she thought later, over supper, should have been that. Except she found herself thinking about what he had said, that one sentence that had sprung out of nothing and led nowhere. He had said that he wanted to get through to her. What had he meant?

She heard herself answering Liz and Gerry's questions, showing the right level of enthusiasm, which really wasn't difficult because it had been a glorious day, but her mind was miles away.

For the first time she contemplated what it was going to be like returning to England and she had a clammy, suffocating feeling of despair. She doubted that she would ever see Angus Hamilton again. Oh, of course, there would be the usual polite parting words about keeping in touch and if she was ever up in London she'd drop by and they could go out for a meal, but she knew that the end of this holiday was the end of it.

Her heart began to beat faster and she stole a glance at him across the table, trying to recapture some of the relief she had felt earlier on at the thought that she would no longer have to be near him and have to cope with the disturbing rollercoaster of emotions which he provoked in her.

I can go back to my life, she told herself unconvincingly. I can get back to reality, because this isn't reality. She wished she could persuade herself that it was a happy prospect, but now, when she thought about it, all she could see was an interminable series of days and weeks and months and years without him around, and she had to struggle to keep a smile on her face when something inside was collapsing. Idiotically.

It was a relief when the meal was finished and the

small talk was done and she no longer had to avoid looking at Angus in case her face revealed too much.

She shut herself in her bedroom, lay on the bed, closed her eyes, opened them, abandoned all hope of sleep, and at a little after midnight slipped into her shorts and T-shirt and made her way to the now totally deserted beach.

She strolled along. There was peace here. The gentle sound of water against coastline, the black sea calm and unruffled. She stood looking out at it and Angus's voice in her ear was such a shock that when she spun around she half expected that it might have been a hallucination. It wasn't.

'Couldn't sleep either?' he asked, standing next to her but not close.

She couldn't look at him. If she looked at him, she would end up drowning, so she stared out to sea and said calmly, while her fingers curled into a ball at her sides and her head spun, 'I must be nervous about the plane trip tomorrow. I was the same before I flew over.'

'Is that it?' he murmured. He took her arm and guided her away from the shoreline and up the beach. He sat down but she remained hovering. 'Sit. I want to talk to you.'

'Do you? What about?' She sat down, but reluctantly, and he turned to face her.

'Look at me.' He held her chin so that she had to look at him and said, as though continuing a conversation which had already been started, 'I was in a foul temper this morning because I didn't want to take you anywhere but I had to.'

'I'm sorry,' Lisa whispered awkwardly, 'but I'm afraid I don't understand. I think we should go inside; it's terribly late.'

'That's exactly what I mean.'

'What?'

'Hasn't anyone ever told you that the faster you run, the harder you'll be chased?' His voice was curt and she stared up at him, wide-eyed and uncomprehending. 'You act like a startled deer caught in someone's headlights, posed to take flight.'

'I'm sorry—' she began, but he interrupted sharply,

'Will you stop apologising? Can you understand what I'm trying to tell you here? I want you, dammit!'

There was a long silence. She continued to stare at him, and she could hear the sound of her heart beating, the sound of the blood in her veins, the sound of her brain trying to come to terms with what he had just said. She wondered whether she might have imagined it.

'No,' she said finally, in a nervous, placating voice, edging away.

Catching her wrist, he grated, 'Stop running away from me.'

'We've been through this,' she murmured weakly, 'We agreed—'

'Nothing. We agreed nothing. Do you imagine that I like being controlled by something as uncontrollable as desire?' He pulled her towards him so that she half fell, and ended up much closer to him than she wanted.

'I don't know what to say.'

'Then don't talk. Just finish what was started.' He curled his fingers into her hair and kissed her without any pretence at gentleness, with a hunger that stirred the flame within her to fire.

Lisa whimpered and tried to turn away and he said huskily, 'Stop trying to fight this thing.' He made it sound as though 'this thing' was somehow monstrous and overwhelming. It was how she felt as well. She had the sensation of being caught in the grip of something that was too big for whatever small defences she had. Desire. Desire as fierce and as savage and as unrelenting as an animal bent on destruction. Desire was what he called it and he should know because he was so much more experienced than she was.

'Tell me that you don't want me,' he groaned against her mouth, and in that instant the promise of what she might have washed away all the caution that existed in her body. She reached up and pulled him towards her, down to the sand, which was dry and powdery under her, kissing him with the same hunger as he had kissed her, a hunger that frightened and excited her in its intensity.

His mouth burnt against her skin and she knew now just how much she had longed for this. Ever since he had kissed her that first time and maybe even before, something inside her had been simmering, waiting for the match to be lit.

She moaned in abandonment as he kissed her face, her neck, turning her head this way and that so that he could caress every bit of exposed skin. He told her, unevenly, that he wanted to touch every part of her body with his mouth and she trembled.

She was not wearing a bra and her breasts ached under the cotton T-shirt. She held his wrist and guided his hand under it and shivered as his palm covered her breast.

He pulled the T-shirt over her head. The breeze on her skin felt good, cooling, and she lay back with her arms outstretched and her eyes half closed, like someone in a trance.

He bent his head and covered her nipple with his mouth, circling it wetly and hungrily, and she arched herself forward, wanting him to absorb more and more of her, until there was nothing left.

When, with her eyes still shut, she felt his hand unzip her shorts, she didn't resist him. She struggled out of them, impatient to return to their lovemaking, hating any interruption, however slight.

This time there was no sharp awakening to reality. This was reality, the only reality that she needed—the here and now.

She parted her legs to accommodate his enquiring fingers and moved against them, barely able to contain herself. In a minute she would no longer be able to fight off the ultimate climax, but he seemed to sense this because he slowed his hand, and slowly licked and kissed her stomach, then her thighs. And she felt his tongue move delicately into the core of her womanhood.

With one hand he continued to stroke her breast, teasing her nipple which was already large and taut with arousal.

She felt her body flinch as he thrust into her.

'I know,' he murmured hoarsely. 'I know. I won't hurt you.'

When he moved inside her again, it was with infinite gentleness, and after a short while her muscles began to relax and she was no longer tense but moaning as his rhythm gathered momentum.

She watched the flat planes of his torso as he moved against her, propped up by one hand while the other massaged her breast, then she closed her eyes and felt waves of pleasure rushing through her, making her ears sing, making her cry out, a hoarse sound in the still, unbroken night. She felt the warm darkness wrap around them like a protective blanket, and she felt a tremendous sense of freedom, of being as light as air. She could have stayed like that for ever.

'Not the most ideal spot for making love,' he said softly into her ear, and she smiled at him.

I love you, she thought. The feeling was so immense that it seemed to take her over. I love you. When did this happen? She ran her fingers through his hair, liking the feel of it slipping through her fingers.

'Absolutely ideal,' she whispered drowsily. 'All black and silver and empty, with nature around us everywhere.'

He laughed, as though the thought hadn't occurred to him.

'What do we do now?' she asked, looking at him. He was all angles and shadows and his eyes glittered in his face.

'We could go back to your room,' he suggested, and she realised with the first stirrings of reality that they were talking at cross purposes. He leaned over her and stroked the side of her face. 'Or we could stay out here surrounded by black and silver nature.' He laughed softly.

She said in a shaky voice, 'No, I mean, what do we do *now*? Where do we go from here? What happens to us?' The magic and romance were beginning to fade, like mist dissipating, but she had to know.

'What do you want to happen?'

'I don't know.' She did know. She wanted to spend the rest of her life with him but she knew without having to be told that that was not a suggestion to be voiced.

'I'm immensely attracted to you,' he murmured, sounding a little surprised.

She watched his powerful arms. 'And you can't understand why.'

'You're not like any of the other women I've gone out with in the past.'

'What sort of women have you gone out with in the past?' She wanted to sit up now and get dressed. The bubble which had surrounded them in that euphoric moment of lovemaking, when she had whimsically imagined that her dreams were about to come true, had burst.

'If I told you, you'd jump to all the wrong conclusions. You'd think that comparisons were being made.'

'Tell me.'

He shrugged, still smiling, still stroking her hair away from her face. 'Very glamorous, very brittle.'

'Like Caroline?'

'Older, but yes, same model, I suppose.'

She sat up and tried not to appear as though she was about to run away. I get the picture, she wanted to say. You're attracted to me, maybe because I'm a different model from the rest, but I do have one vital thing in common with your queue of glamorous, brittle blondes, haven't I? I'm just passing through.

'I want to see you when we get back to England,' he said softly.

'For how long?' she enquired.

'Who knows? We may get thoroughly sick of each other after a week.' He was teasing her, but she wasn't about to be teased. His words had a chilling element of truth behind them. What he wanted was sex, until she had been weaned out of his system. No talk of commitment, certainly no talk of love.

But I love you, she thought, and I don't know if I can be with you for one week or two or a month or six months, never knowing when the end will come. It was like travelling with her parents all over again. The same insecurity, the same rootlessness. It wasn't what she wanted.

'London's a long way from Reading,' she told him.

'I have a very fast car.'

She slipped on her T-shirt with shaking fingers, feeling the sand against her skin with sudden distaste, then she stood up and began putting on the rest of her clothes.

'What's the matter?' he asked sharply, also standing up and getting dressed, and she shrugged, 'Are you going to tell me or am I going to have to play guessing games with you?'

'Nothing's the matter.'

'You've switched off,' he said, with an edge to his voice. 'One minute you're opening up to me and the next minute you've retreated behind those walls of yours again. Now, are you going to tell me what's wrong or am I going to have to shake it out of you?'

She began walking off. She didn't trust herself to speak. She didn't want to do anything stupid like break down and she certainly wasn't about to confess undying love and risk losing what little was left of her pride.

'Answer me, dammit!' His fingers curled round her wrist and he pulled her round to face him.

She looked at him mutely, which only seemed to sharpen the edge of his anger. Her hand lay limply in the grip of his fingers and she stabbed her toes into the sand, making a little mound like a molehill.

'I can't...' She began helplessly, not looking at him. 'I just can't get involved in a relationship where I'm at the beck and call of someone else. I spent years being at the beck and call of my parents and I can't go through that again.'

'We are not talking about the same thing here.'

'Not the same, no,' she agreed, 'but similar.'

'This is ridiculous.'

Her head snapped up and she glared at him with eyes which were filling up with tears and which would betray her, she knew, if she allowed it.

'For you, maybe, but not for me. That's the way I feel and there's nothing more to be said.'

'And what happened between us?' he asked tightly. 'No more to be said on that either?'

'I enjoyed it...' Lisa muttered. She dashed her hand across her eyes angrily, because he was forcing her to say things that she didn't want to say and which her ears didn't want to hear. She didn't need to be reminded of how much she had wanted him because it would only show her how much she still did.

'But enjoyment is not enough—not without your precious guarantees.'

More silence. The mound at her feet was growing and she flattened it back down.

'Fine,' he said abruptly. 'We'll just write the whole episode off.' He released her and she stumbled away from him without looking back, away from the treacherous night breeze that had felt like a caress against her skin only an hour before but which now felt like ice.

She let herself into her room, had a shower, got into the oversized T-shirt which she slept in. Her movements were automatic. There was only room in her brain for one thing. Angus. He usurped every other thought. His presence filled the room, filled her head, filled her body until she wanted to scream, which of course she couldn't do, so instead she covered herself with the blankets and stuffed her face into the pillow, and was trying to force herself to think of something else, *anything* else, when she felt a touch on her shoulder.

She surfaced from under the layers of bedlinen and

saw a figure sitting on the edge of her bed, and she opened her mouth to scream.

'It's me,' Angus hissed at her. 'Shh...' He put his hand across her mouth and she stared up at him, dumbfounded.

'I've been thinking,' he said accusingly, with his hand still over her mouth, as though now he had calmed her he still didn't want her to say anything.

'Mmm,' Lisa contributed against the palm of his hand. Her fingers curled into the sheet and she had the feeling that if she blinked he would dematerialise.

'I don't care to be blackmailed.'

I was not blackmailing you! she wanted to yell, but again all she could do was mutter something incoherent, and she made another attempt to pull his hand away.

'Not yet.' He paused and raked his hair back in a frustrated gesture. 'I think your attitude is puritanical and misguided.'

Lisa grunted angrily in disagreement.

'But,' he continued, 'since you don't seem prepared to change it, I propose you move in with me.' He removed his hand and for a second she didn't say a word. Not a word. For a second there, when he had said 'I propose', she had insanely jumped to the wrong conclusion. The rest of his suggestion sank in like a stone into cold water. What he proposed was still the same—sex on his terms but with the boundary lines slightly altered. It wasn't commitment.

'I am not,' she said in a deadly calm voice, when her vocal cords finally loosened up enough for her to say anything at all, 'moving in with you. I am not going to be your mistress.'

'Why not?' he asked in a low, furious voice that made her cringe back against the pillow. 'What do you want?'

There was a tense silence, then he said curtly, 'Marriage? Is that it?' And when she didn't answer he carried on relentlessly, 'Marriage is not for me. I've seen the downside of marriage; I've watched my parents stay married, or should I say tied to one another, for no better reason than it was a habit easier to keep than to break.' He leaned over her, dark, threatening, angry, his hands on either side of her body.

'You say that life has no guarantees,' she whispered. 'Does it automatically follow that because your parents' marriage was a bad one, then your marriage, if ever you do decide to marry, would follow the same course? My parents had an extremely close marriage.'

'There is no room for debate on the subject, Lisa.'

'And children?' she flung at him.

'Are for other people and good luck to them. God damn you, woman, I am offering you as much commitment as I've ever offered any woman. Take it!'

'Go,' she said, turning her head so that she didn't have to look at him. 'Leave me alone. I don't want what you're offering.'

She could feel his eyes burning into her but she refused to meet them. As far as she was concerned, there was nothing left to say. He had laid down his terms and they weren't good enough. Sure, he might be handing out the most he was capable of giving in the line of commitment, but it wasn't enough.

Did he expect her to abandon everything so she could spend an indefinite length of time, because she had no idea of where his boredom threshold lay, living on a knife-edge?

He pushed himself off the bed and stood towering above her for a few seconds.

'So be it,' he said, then he walked towards the door

and left, slamming it behind him, and only then did she fall back against the pillows with the sickish feeling of having been put through a wringer. Her head was spinning. She was quite sure that if she tried to climb out of bed she would fall down.

She wished that she had had the sense to lock the bedroom door. If she had he would have had to bang on it to be let in and she would not have answered. She would not have had to listen to what was, in the end, the final insult. However much he was attracted to her, for reasons which she still couldn't pin down, he would never marry her; he would never give her the one thing she needed.

She lay on the bed with her eyes wide open and stared upwards at the ceiling, which she didn't see. Her eyes were blind to everything except what was going on in her mind.

He had told her that he didn't believe in marriage, that it was an institution which had no place in his life. She wondered whether he was being truthful. She wondered whether the real reason why he would never marry her was far more fundamental than that.

She was of a different social background—the most basic difference which Caroline had put her finger on almost immediately, and which she had made no bones about hiding.

She didn't honestly imagine that he would remain a bachelor all his life, but when he did marry it would be to someone with a suitable pedigree.

How dared he call her puritanical and misguided, just because she happened to have a few principles?

It was a shame that her principles hadn't jumped to the rescue earlier, on the beach, she thought, but really, making love with him was something she didn't regret.

If she had turned her back on him and walked away, she would have spent a lifetime wondering.

He had held out his hand and she had taken it; she had willingly let him lead her into a whole new, bright world which she had never known existed.

Somehow, though, she knew that living with him would be a humiliating experience. She would never be able to relax because she would never know how much longer he would be around. And when the time came for her to walk away it would be a shabby, disillusioned parting. No, it made her sick just thinking about it.

Better this way, she told herself. It seems hellish but there are fewer pieces to pick up now than there would be six months down the road.

She closed her eyes and let sleep take over.

CHAPTER SIX

IT WAS cold and dark and raining when the plane landed at Heathrow airport.

Lisa stared out of the window of the taxi and watched the water slide along the glass. She didn't want to think of that trip back, but it was as though her mind had reached an impenetrable barrier and her thoughts could not stretch beyond it.

Angus had not said a word to her for the entire journey. He had barely glanced in her direction. He had sat next to Gerry on the plane, and from behind them she had heard the low murmur of their voices and had miserably fed off the sound of his dark, deep tones, filled with an unspeakable yearning.

The taxi finally cleared the congested airport traffic and began picking up speed on the motorway. The taxi driver's earlier attempts at conversation had met with such blank unresponsiveness that he had eventually given up, but she gathered that it had been raining nonstop more or less for the fortnight that she had been away. Dull grey skies and constant rain that made everyone scurry along the pavements with their umbrellas up and their expressions pinched.

By the time they made it back to her flat, sun and sand and sea seemed like a distant dream. At the time, she had thought the holiday was winding along very slowly. Now she realised that it had shot past like a bullet.

'In a week's time,' Paul told her knowledgeably the

following day when she turned up for work, 'you'll have a look at the photos and it'll seem like a year ago. Ellie keeps telling me that the only way round that is to book another holiday the minute the last one's finished.'

Lisa smiled at him in passing. He had missed her. The paperwork hadn't been done and some of their customers had been asking after her.

She should have felt pleased and relieved to be back among the tubs and plants and dwarf conifers, but she didn't. She had a dreadful feeling of unreality, as though she had stepped back into a life that was now in some way out of kilter.

Two weeks later, when the holiday snapshots arrived through the letterbox, she sat down and looked at them over and over again and realised that what Paul had said was true. The reality of winter had put a stranglehold on her imagination. She found it hard to recapture the memory of blistering sunshine and long, lazy days.

Routine and the humdrum business of living made two weeks of escapism seem like a mirage. If she thought too hard about it, it would all suddenly disappear and she would realise that she had been nowhere at all.

Except, she thought, if that was the case, Angus would have faded into a blurry, distant image as well, a memory neatly stored away at the back of her mind. And he hadn't.

It was so unfair. She was trying so hard to forget, but his image lurked so close to the surface, waiting to spring out at her like an intruder. She could confine every area of her life but she couldn't seem to confine her thoughts at all. One stray memory would creep into her head when she was least expecting it and then it would proliferate until it became a network of memories, strangling the imposed orderliness of her mind like an onslaught of ivy devouring a wall.

The strain of pretending to the world that she was the same person she had been before was so tiring that it was nearly six weeks before some little thought process in her head registered something that made her go cold with fear.

She had missed a period.

She was sitting with her book on her lap and a cup of coffee balanced precariously on her thigh, when everything seemed to shut down inside her. Nearly a month late. She hadn't even thought about it before; she had been too busy trying to get her life back in order.

The following morning she went to the pharmacy, bought herself a kit and watched with a clammy feeling as a thin blue line impersonally informed her that her life was never going to be the same again. She was pregnant.

I can't be, she thought, staring at the little plastic tester as though it were something alien, but she couldn't even begin to pretend to herself that it was wrong, that she had somehow fed it the right ingredients and had been handed back an incorrect answer.

She sat down on the edge of her sofa with her head in her hands and felt ill.

She had never thought that this could happen to her; it hadn't once crossed her mind when she had lain there, on the beach, and made love to a man she was destined never to see again.

She started to laugh hysterically, until the tears came to her eyes, and then, with shock, she realised that she was no longer laughing but crying. How could she have been so stupid? She, of all people? She could remember the talk her parents had given her about the birds and the bees. It had been more of a biological discussion about reproduction and she could remember her mother saying, 'You might not think that it will ever happen to you, but it will and it's as well to be prepared if you don't want an accident to happen.'

Well, the accident had happened, except it was more of a catastrophe than an accident.

She lay down on the sofa with her eyes shut and the enormity of what had happened spread over her until she thought she was being engulfed.

Why me? she asked herself. She was forever reading in the newspapers about couples who couldn't have children, who had had to resort to fertility treatment. It had never crossed her mind that she could fall pregnant as a result of one ill-timed moment of passion.

What was she going to do?

The following morning, dry-eyed, she confronted Paul in his office and told him without any preamble.

'I'm afraid I have some surprising news.' She had to hold onto the edge of his desk because she could feel the ground swaying under her feet. 'I'm going to have a baby.'

There was a thick silence and she didn't dare lift her eyes to his because she could imagine the shock on his face. It wouldn't have been so bad if she hadn't been such an intensely private person, so in control of her life, the sort of person that these kinds of things just didn't happen to.

'You don't look over the moon about it.'

She finally lifted her eyes and saw the surprise still there, unconvincingly camouflaged under a show of cheery *bonhomie*.

'You're a dark horse, Lisa,' he said. 'I didn't even think there was a man in your life.'

'There isn't,' she replied shortly, then she regretted the abruptness of her answer because she could understand how he was feeling. Over the years they had developed a closeness of sorts and it would be as though he had misread her personality altogether.

'It just happened,' she said wearily, sitting down, 'and I'm not sure what I'm going to do.'

'Nothing rash, I hope.' He looked at her sympathetically, which made her feel like crying, and reached out and squeezed her hand. 'It's not the end of the world, you know,' he said awkwardly, but with feeling. 'Your job here's safe. Is there any chance that the father...?'

'No.' Her head shot up. 'He doesn't know and he won't. This is my problem.' She remembered Angus telling her that children were for other people and good luck to them. Unnecessary clutter, his voice had implied and he had swiftly moved on. It was a subject on which he had probably never dwelled and had no intention of doing so.

'Thanks for, you know, reassuring me about the job,' she said, clearing her head of unwanted thoughts.

'Is there anyone you can tell? Any family at all?'

'No one.' It sounded forlorn, said like that, but it was true. There was no one, and the loneliness of her situation forced its way on her with a great wave of despair. Friends would rally round, she knew, but it would never be the same as having family support. In the end, she would be on her own. On her own with a pregnancy she didn't want, on her own with a baby, on her own with every imaginable responsibility, although she told herself that she wasn't the only person to have found herself in this kind of situation.

'Ellie will help out, you know that...' he said gently, and she didn't answer. Ellie, his wife, was a dear. She had three children of her own, but like Paul she would be shocked at the news, shocked that the unimaginable had happened. As would everyone she worked with. They would all find out in due course. She would become a topic of conversation and, even if it wasn't malicious conversation, the private part of her was dismayed at the prospect.

But it eased her mind to know that her job was safe, and over the next three months she added a few more tenuous silver linings to the cloud. She had a roof over her head, and she had a few good friends.

They had all been sympathetic, they had all hidden their curiosity about the paternity of the baby with a great deal of compassionate understanding, and they were all quite excited on her behalf.

She needed it because she felt next to no excitement at all. She just felt sick most of the time and tired the rest, and anxious.

She was beginning to show and occasionally she would glance down at her growing stomach with a certain amount of wonder at what was happening inside there, out of sight. When she did that, she did feel protective, but there was no counting of days on the calendar or strolling through baby shops excitedly planning what to buy. That, she thought, was more appropriate for women with partners, both sharing the joy of a new life in the making.

It wasn't for her. She just continued feeling vulnerable. In due course, when the time came nearer, she would buy things for the baby, but not yet.

Summer was beginning to fade, with the blue skies becoming rarer every day and the nights drawing in, when Paul suggested an outing to a flower show. It would be quite an honour to attend because it was the first of its kind. Displays of selected flowers only, rare species, hybrids. Two complimentary tickets had been sent to them.

'I can't go,' he explained, 'because I'll be abroad, but you go and take a friend. You'll enjoy it. It'll make a change from here.'

Lisa looked at his kind, open face with gratitude. He had been marvellous about the whole thing, encouraging her when she seemed low and having her over to dinner at least once a week, ostensibly so that she could see a bit of family life at first hand but really because he felt sorry for her.

'I thought you wanted me here to cover for you while you were in Germany,' she said, and he waved his hand airily.

'I think the place can spare you for a day,' he said. 'Have a day out. It'll do you good.'

So three days later she set off for London under strict instructions to have a damn good time and see if she could sniff out any bargains that they might want to stock for the following summer.

The place, when she arrived, was jammed. The big flower shows, she knew, were always packed, but she had not expected quite such a crowd for what was, after all, an élite event with only certain categories of flowers and plants on display.

At the entrance, she thought that she would never make it, not having to contend with throngs of people pushing against her when all she really felt like doing was having a long sleep, but once she was inside the crowd thinned out and she began to have a proper, thorough look at everything.

There were roses, but peculiarly shaped ones or else unusually coloured ones, and there was any number of foreign flora, with their wild, exotic hues strangely amplified by the ordinary surroundings.

The huge hall was filled with heady, sweet scents and the sounds of people exclaiming over something or other. She had taken a little notebook with her and as she stopped in front of each plant she sized it up with a view to possible stocking, and took the appropriate notes.

She was being swept along on the tide of people moving from one display to the next, when she picked up the well-bred tones of one voice, and as her head snapped around their eyes met through the crowd and Lisa had a swaying feeling, as if she was about to fall.

She heard a woman say, 'Are you all right, dear?'

She nodded distractedly, about to push on, when Caroline's voice said from next to her, 'What a surprise. Lisa something or other, isn't it?'

'Freeman.'

She could feel the blood soaring through her and she had the same giddy feeling she used to have now and again, earlier on in her pregnancy, when she suddenly stood up and felt the ground swaying gently under her feet.

'Yes, of course. I'd forgotten.' Caroline's face was as tanned as it had been when they had returned from the West Indies and she was wearing a glamorous green trouser outfit which seemed far more appropriate to a cocktail party than a garden exhibition, but Lisa could remember that about her choice of clothes. They were never casual. They always seemed just a little too grand for the occasion.

'How are you, Caroline?' she asked faintly. At least her voice sounded all right, but she knew that her knuckles were white and her hands were tightly balled into fists at her sides.

'Just fine.' The green, feline eyes swept over her, and she said, smiling, but with an unpleasant undertone, 'I see that congratulations are in order.'

Did I really think that she might not notice? Lisa thought. She felt sick as though the air had suddenly become too hot and was pressing down upon her, making her sweat.

'Thank you.'

'And how many months?'

'A little over four.' She tried to smile, as though this were routine stuff for her—a few pleasantries with a passing acquaintance—but she could feel the tension in her body like a rush of freezing water through her veins.

'I see.' Caroline looked at her with those hard, glittering eyes. 'And where is your husband? Here with you?' she asked, and Lisa didn't answer. What was there to say?

'Are you enjoying the display?' she eventually asked, a little wildly.

'Usual dull affair,' Caroline answered. 'Here with Mummy, actually. She's terribly involved in this sort of thing and she dragged me along to help out.'

'Well…I hope you have a nice time.' Good heavens, what pointless small talk, when all I want to do is get away and hope that she doesn't put two and two together, she thought. 'I really must be going…'

'I tried my luck with Angus, you know, but he wasn't interested. I think you were right when you said that he saw me as an underage minor—despite my attempts to persuade him otherwise.' She was smiling, the same repellent, cold smile that frightened Lisa. 'But in a way I'm jolly glad nothing came of it. He said that he was utterly uninterested in any kind of long-term relationship with any woman. He was terribly polite about it. I personally think that that sort of thing would cramp his lifestyle, don't you agree?'

Lisa shrugged.

'Dear Angus moves in the fast lane,' she continued. 'Wouldn't it be a shame if he had to slow down because of some disaster? I mean...' She leaned forward confidentially. Lisa felt the brush of the green silk against her arm. 'Here's a thought... You're a little over four months pregnant. He could be the father, couldn't he? If you two had had a fling... Not that I'm saying you did! But the timing's there, isn't it?

'Do you know, if the Press ever discovered that he had fathered an illegitimate child and not taken responsibility, they would have a field day? He has such a high profile, and some of his largest advertising campaigns are quite morally based. What a thought.

'Still...' she appeared to give this some thought '...I personally would find it very amusing if he was brought down a peg or two. Rejection isn't a word I understand.'

'I'm sure you don't mean that, Caroline,' Lisa said with growing horror at the implications of what the other woman had said. 'I'm sure you're not a vindictive person.'

'Of course I'm not! But there's always something a little sweet about revenge, isn't there? You never said, by the way—are you married?'

Someone jostled her from behind. Lisa had never felt so grateful to an inconsiderate, passing stranger in all her life.

'I really must get on,' she said, bravely meeting Caroline's eyes and not looking away. 'I'm being pushed by people who want to have a look at your mother's display. Do congratulate her from me. It's a beautiful selection of flowers.'

She wouldn't have guessed that she could be so articulate when her mind was whirling around like a spinning top, going faster and faster.

'I will, yes, of course.' Caroline stepped back and offered her profile for inspection. 'And I shall also tell her how glad I am that I was forced into coming here. After all, how else would we have met? And I'm so glad that we did. Aren't you?'

There was no point in even trying to enjoy the flowers now, but she trudged through the rest of the displays, taking notes, even though the blooms had all merged into one great, gaudy mass of colour.

By the time she made it back to her flat, she was spent. Her mind played and replayed that conversation with Caroline. Every way she looked at it, from whatever angle, she couldn't escape or misread the insinuations behind the words. Caroline wanted her revenge on Angus. She had made a pass at him and had been courteously turned down and rejection, as she had said herself, was not a concept she found easy to swallow. What better revenge now than to see him forced into a fatherhood he didn't want?

She didn't sleep that night. Normally, the minute her head hit the pillow she was out like a light, but not now. She tossed and turned and created a thousand and one scenarios in her mind and then unconvincingly tried to tell herself that she was being foolish, that Caroline's words had been no more than a vindictive threat.

But it hardly worked. She was, she realised by the end of the week, waiting. Waiting for the phone to ring, standing on the edge of a precipice, waiting to fall.

By the end of two weeks, she was beginning to hope

that he had maybe lost her address somewhere, and he would never find her through the phone book because she was ex-directory. She tried desperately to remember if she had mentioned where she worked, but for the life of her she couldn't.

By the end of three weeks, she no longer looked at the telephone with the wariness of someone expecting the worst.

Autumn had now pushed the last vestiges of summer away. The leaves on the trees were beginning to turn red and gold and fall to the ground. She extracted her waterproof jacket and her coat from cold storage, only to realise that they would never last the course of the pregnancy. In fact, not many of her clothes still did fit her. She had had to carefully fold her jeans and put them away and now she began sewing some maternity clothes, which she did without joy, simply with the determined knowledge that she had to. She couldn't afford the luxury of buying an entire wardrobe of maternity wear.

She stopped worrying about Angus because no news was good news. She stopped dwelling obsessively on that conversation with Caroline because if she was going to create trouble then she would have done so by now. She also stopped jumping every time the phone went and then tiptoeing to answer it, as if one false move and it would attack, like something out of a tacky horror movie.

On a cold, blustery Friday evening, she heard the doorbell ring and went to answer it without a second thought.

Her friend Judy had taken to calling round at the end of the week. Sometimes they went out for a cheap meal, but more often than not they just sat and chatted.

Her shock on seeing Angus standing outside her front

door was so profound that she felt her entire body stiffen, as though someone had waved a magic wand and turned her into stone.

She stared at him without saying anything. Shock had not galvanised her into action. It had done the opposite. It had deprived her of her power of speech; it had thickened her mind so that she could hardly think; it had frozen every nerve in her body.

She had been wrong. She had not remembered everything about him. She had forgotten, for a start, how intensely powerful his presence was, how the arrogant sweep of his dark features gave him a brooding, mesmerising look. She had forgotten that peculiar, penetrating clarity of his eyes, the deepest of blues that revealed nothing.

'Surprised, Lisa?'

'What are you doing here?' At least she could speak now, even though it was only in a whisper. At least she could think even though her thoughts were flying around in her head like a swarm of bees unexpectedly released.

'What do you think?' There was no lazy charm in his face. His mouth was a narrow line and he wasn't smiling. She knew that what she was seeing was the cold, hard steel beneath the velvet. 'Aren't you going to ask me inside?'

He didn't wait for an answer. He reached out and pushed the door back and stepped inside, leaving her to shut the door behind her and stand there, with her hands behind her back. He didn't look around him. He turned and faced her, with his hands in his pockets.

Now that her nightmares had finally materialised, she found that she didn't have a clue what to do, what to say. She stared at him mutely and he gave her a savage, cold smile.

'Haven't you got your little speech ready, Lisa?'

'What little speech? What are you talking about?' Her heart was beating so fast that it felt as though it would burst at any moment.

'Did you think that I wouldn't come around?' he asked, with the same cold, cruel smile on his mouth. 'Were you beginning to worry that your little plan might go astray?'

'What little plan? What are you talking about?'

'Don't play games with me!' he bellowed, and she cringed back against the door, grateful for the support it gave her.

'I've been away in America. Caroline was waiting for me the day after I got back.'

Lisa walked shakily into the living room, across to the sofa and sat down with her hands on her lap. So it hadn't been an empty threat after all. Had she really imagined that it had been? What an optimistic fool. Caroline was not the sort to make empty threats, not when she could taste the honeyed sweetness of revenge.

'I see.'

'I'm sure you do.' His mouth twisted into a cynical sneer. 'And there's really no need to go on acting the innocent with me. Just tell me how much money you want.'

'Money?' She looked up at him with utter bewilderment.

'Yes, money. Or were you hoping that I would skirt round the subject in a more tactful way? When you cut through the waffle, it has such a nasty ring, hasn't it?'

'I don't know what you're talking about. I won't be bullied by you in my own house.'

'When did you devise your little plan, Lisa?' he asked in a dangerously soft voice.

'Angus, please...'

'Angus, please...what?'

'What did Caroline say to you?'

'What did Caroline say to me? What didn't she say to me would be nearer the target. She told me that she was at the flower show, helping her mother, when you confronted her. She said that you couldn't wait to tell her that you were pregnant by me and that you would make sure I paid through the nose for sleeping with you when there was nothing in it for you.'

Lisa's face whitened.

'None of that's true,' she whispered.

'So tell me, when did you decide to play your trump card? Did you lead me on until you knew that making love would result in a pregnancy?' He stepped towards her and she stared at him with wide-eyed horror. 'A bit of a gamble, wasn't it? I suppose you figured that you had nothing to lose, though, didn't you? If it didn't work, if you didn't fall pregnant, then you would slide back into obscurity. If you did, then all you had to do was engineer the right moment to meet Caroline, and that would be the easy part.

'Clever of you to remember that her mother exhibited flowers. All it would have needed was a phone call to see whether she would be there on the same day as you, and if that didn't work, then you could always bump into her somewhere else. Accidentally, of course.'

'No! You're not making any sense!'

'Am I not?'

'I had no idea that Caroline would be there! I didn't phone to find out anything! I don't know how you have the nerve to come into my house and accuse me of things...like that!' Her voice had begun to waver and she had to grit her teeth together so that she didn't break down and start crying. She took a deep breath.

He raked his fingers through his hair and stared at her with a mixture of anger and doubt and sheer frustration. Then he began to pace the room, his movements restless.

'It is mine, I take it?'

'Yes.'

He paused in front of her and said darkly, 'I won't be blackmailed into anything, I can tell you that right now. You say that you didn't engineer a meeting with Caroline…'

'And I didn't confront her either!' Lisa looked at him resentfully. 'She confronted *me*! I wasn't even supposed to be at that flower show but Paul couldn't make it and he wanted me to go along and make notes. By the time I saw her, it was too late to… She guessed at once. She was elated. She said that she had tried to…that she had…'

She couldn't formulate the thought and she couldn't tell whether he understood her meaning or not because he continued to look at her with that opaque, unreadable look that was so frightening.

'She said that she wanted to make you pay for rejecting her.' There, it was out, and she met his stare with bright, stubborn eyes.

'And why should I believe you?' he asked coolly.

'I don't care if you don't!'

There was a thick silence, then he said, with less rage but no more warmth, 'I'm going now, but I promise you I'll be back.' He turned around and walked out, slamming the door behind him, and she collapsed back against the sofa. Now that she was alone, the unshed tears refused to come.

She sat there while the gloom gathered around her and

thought about every word he had said. She thought about the savage anger on his face as he had hurled those accusations at her. She knew that she shouldn't be surprised, that Caroline was just the sort of girl who would feel no compunction about twisting the truth into something that she could make into a blunt instrument and use for her own benefit. But it still hurt that he could have accepted her as gold-digger so easily.

How could he have thought she would use him as a passport to money?

She fell asleep on the sofa and awoke with stiff joints the following day. It was just as well that it was the weekend and she didn't have to go to work. Her body ached.

She put her hand on her stomach and thought that the only sensible thing was happening there inside her, and then it occurred to her, with surprise, that over the past few months, while she had been busily saving her money and working out how she was going to cope with a baby, some part of her had slowly become used to the idea and that same part of her now felt more than protective about this child. It had moved from being a catastrophe to something which she now accepted and wanted very badly.

She went and did her shopping and later, just after she had finished her meal, Paul dropped by. He was literally just passing in front of her house, and wanted to tell her that lunch the following day was off. Timothy had chickenpox and it now looked as though the other two were getting it. Ellie had spotted one sinister red bump on Jenny's stomach and had gloomily predicted that it would have grown into several hundred by morning.

Lisa smiled and listened, cheered up by this mundane

conversation when she had spent the whole day in a state of heightened emotional upheaval.

'We don't want you getting ill,' Paul said, smiling and patting her hand. 'Not,' he added with a wicked grin, 'when winter stock is being delivered on Monday and you have to be there to supervise.'

'Oh, I see,' Lisa laughed. 'So much for my welfare.'

'Just joking.'

'I know that!' They continued chatting for a few minutes about their supply of shrubs, quite a few of which had been delivered three days previously and now seemed to be substandard, and he was just getting up to leave when the doorbell went.

Lisa was still smiling when she opened the door. The sight of Angus standing outside drained the smile away from her face and she felt all the familiar apprehension flooding through her again. Every time she saw him, he seemed taller and leaner than she remembered, and more threatening. She remained standing in front of the open doorway, and followed the line of his eyes as they flicked past her to where Paul was slipping on his jacket.

'Come at a bad time, have I?' he asked cynically.

Paul was now standing behind her, and before she could make any introductions Angus said in a cold, tight voice that contained an element of aggression. 'And you are…?'

'Paul Waterman. Lisa works for me.' He extended his hand and Angus looked down at it, ignored it and then raised cool eyes back to Paul's now slightly confused face.

'Really. And calling in here comes under the heading of good staff relations, does it?'

Lisa went bright red and automatically linked her arm through Paul's, an unconscious gesture of protectiveness which didn't escape Angus's attention. His eyes narrowed and he said tightly, 'If you're on your way out, then we won't keep you.'

'I'll decide when my visitors leave, thank you,' she interrupted in a high voice. Her face was flushed and angry.

'I was on my way out, actually,' Paul said stiffly, 'and I'm afraid you still haven't introduced yourself. You are...?'

'Hamilton. Angus Hamilton.' It was the barest of concessions to politeness because his eyes remained hard and glittering.

Paul turned to her and said amiably, 'Sorry about tomorrow, Lisa.'

'Let me know how the children are,' she said with affection, 'and if there's anything at all I can do...'

He smiled, nodded and left, edging past Angus as though he found his presence as alarming as she did, and as soon as he was out of the house Angus turned to her and said icily, 'What a cosy relationship. And what exactly would you do for him? How far do your services extend?'

He brushed past her and she reluctantly shut the door and followed him through. Without the benefit of knowledge, anyone might have said that his reaction to Paul had been the reaction of a jealous man, but she knew the truth, and the truth solidified the little ball of misery sitting in the pit of her stomach.

He didn't care who Paul Waterman was. His caustic question wasn't the fierce interrogation of a jealous lover, it was the caustic enquiry of a man who thought she would do anything for money.

'Well?' he snapped, facing her across the small living room. 'You haven't answered my question. Does that man make a habit of visiting you when you're on your own?'

'*That man*,' Lisa replied, determined not to cower in the face of his formidable presence, 'is my boss and we have a wonderful working relationship. He stopped by to tell me that his invitation for lunch tomorrow has been postponed because his children have come down with chickenpox. There was no need for you to be rude to him.'

She expected him to respond with something cool and cutting but he flushed and turned away, moving to sit down on the sofa.

'Can you blame me?' he asked harshly, but with a look of angry discomfort on his face which she found a little confusing, simply because he was a man whose self-control never slipped. 'You tell me that you didn't fall pregnant on purpose, yet it's an uncanny coincidence that we make love once and it happens. And you blind me with this innocent portrayal of yourself, all girlish blushing and stammering timidity, yet I come here unexpectedly and there's a man in your house, a man whose company you clearly enjoy because you were smiling when you came to the door.'

'Oh, what's the use?' she said with a sigh. 'What's the good of defending myself? You won't believe me anyway. You've already made up your mind about what sort of person I am, so why don't you just tell me why you've come here?'

'I've come here,' he said, as though challenging her to make something of it, 'to apologise.'

CHAPTER SEVEN

'I WENT to see Caroline,' Angus said evenly, 'and I got the truth out of her. She told me that events hadn't occurred quite as she originally narrated them. Obviously I was way out of line when I accused you of manipulation.

He was leaning forward, his elbows resting on his thighs, his fingers loosely entwined.

'I see,' Lisa said coldly.

'Is that the extent of your reaction?' he asked tautly, and she averted her face.

'How would you like me to react? Would you like me to shout with relief that you no longer see me as the avaricious gold-digger you accused me of being yesterday? Is that what you'd like?' She turned to face him, her eyes flashing. 'Well, I hate to say this but it hardly changes the insult implied when you levelled those accusations at me in the first place.'

'I take your point,' he replied tersely, 'but you have to understand that I'm in the direct firing line for any woman who gets it in her head that her lifestyle needs improving, I'm very good at spotting the danger signs a mile off. Naturally when Caroline ran to me with her tale I wondered whether you had been the one to slip through the net.'

'Fine.' She shrugged and waited for him to continue. She didn't see why she should make things any easier for him and it occurred to her that she would have to develop a bit more backbone as far as he was concerned, if she was to find the strength to fight him on her own ground.

She couldn't continue seeing him through the eyes of a lovestruck girl. This was no longer simply a question of her. There was the baby to consider now, too.

'Would you care to offer me a cup of coffee?' he asked eventually, and she glanced across at him suspiciously, as though suspecting there might be some further, carefully concealed attack lurking behind the perfectly ordinary request. She wasn't about to fall into the trap of trusting him. She had seen the depths of his rage beneath the civilised veneer, and that, she thought, would be a constant reminder to her that the real man beneath the sophisticated, urbane glamour was as ruthless and dangerous as a jungle animal.

'I would have,' she said politely, standing up, 'but I didn't realise that you intended to stay long enough to drink it.'

He followed her into the kitchen and said to her averted back, 'We have to talk.'

'I suppose so,' she answered reluctantly. She poured the hot water into the mugs and her hand was trembling. So much, she thought, for that passing bravado. She wasn't looking at him, but she could feel his presence in the kitchen and it made her nervous and jumpy. She had to force herself to control her face so that when she turned round to proffer the mug to him her expression was blank and composed.

She followed him back into the living room, took the chair facing his and eyed him silently over the rim of her mug.

'Would you ever have told me?' He crossed his legs, ankle resting on knee, and regarded her.

'I don't know. Maybe one day.' She frowned. 'No,

probably not,' she admitted. 'I can't see that there would ever have been the need to.'

He very slowly rested the mug on the table in front of him and then said coldly, 'No need? No need to inform a child of the identity of its father?'

'No,' she said, nervously aware that she wasn't saying the right things. 'Look, I have no intention of upsetting your life.' She paused and tried to think how to proceed from here without treading on any mines.

'Let's move on from there, shall we?' he countered in a hard voice. 'Let's begin with the assumption that my life is already, as you put it, upset.'

'In that case, there's no need for it to be upset further. I just want you to know that I'm not going to try and force you into taking any responsibility for this. It was a mistake. I wasn't thinking straight; I never imagined I would get pregnant.'

'So, ideally, I should just walk right out of that door and not look back, is that it?'

'Yes. That would be for the best, I think.'

'Oh, it would, would it?' There was cold cynicism in his voice, making her hot and nervous.

'I think so, don't you? I mean, this is my responsibility. It doesn't have anything to do with you.'

'*Your* responsibility!' he bellowed furiously. 'Nothing to do with me!'

'Of course,' Lisa said hurriedly, 'I know that you're *responsible*. Technically, that is. But what I'm trying to tell you is that I have no intention of making any demands on you or having this interfere with your life.'

'How thoughtful of you.' His mouth curled derisively.

'Yes, I think so!' she snapped with hostility. 'I can't win, can I? First I'm accused of getting pregnant so that

I can blackmail you, then I'm accused of doing just the opposite!'

'You're being deliberately obtuse.'

'I am not!'

'You're avoiding the truth of the situation because it suits you to do so and you expect me to fall into line.'

'And what *is* the truth of the situation?' She was perched on the edge of the chair, and now she sat back and tried to get a grip on her emotions. This sort of arguing couldn't be good for the baby. She placed her hand on her stomach and felt it kicking. Was it her imagination or was it kicking more than usual? Was it picking up vibes, or responding to all the high voices and the surge of feeling running through her blood?

She wished that she had never laid eyes on him again. In fact, she wished that he had never entered her un-cluttered, uncomplicated life. Why couldn't he accept that she was doing him a favour by not disrupting his life with an unwanted baby? He lived his life at break-neck speed. There was no room in that sort of life for any relationship other than the most transient and babies were not transient creatures. They were demanding, vo-racious human beings who didn't need occasional, dis-ruptive appearances from a man who was technically a father but in reality more of a stranger.

'The truth is that you bitterly regret what happened between us and you expect me to vanish conveniently off the face of the earth so that you can put the whole unfortunate episode behind you. Sadly for you, I'm not about to oblige. This isn't about you. I happen to have some stakes here too. Just a few. About fifty per cent.'

'I'm going to be bringing up this baby,' she said stiffly. 'I know that you mean well...'

'But...?' he asked cynically. 'You can manage quite happily on your own?'

Lisa didn't say anything. She looked down stubbornly at her fingers, her mouth set. There didn't seem to be much point in arguing with him. Whichever way she turned, he found a door and slammed it in her face.

'Well?' he persisted, and she shrugged and muttered, 'That's right.'

'How much money do you earn?'

'Money has nothing to do with it!' she told him hotly. 'What difference does it make how much money I earn? Does it follow that if I lived in a big house with a big garden and took expensive holidays every year I would somehow make a better mother? Do you think that money buys everything? If you do, then I feel sorry for you!'

'How much?' The hard blue eyes looked at her steadily and she grudgingly told him what he wanted to know. It didn't matter anyway. She was in the right on this.

'And you honestly don't believe that it would make the slightest difference if I accepted responsibility and allowed this baby to benefit from my wealth?'

'I don't want any of your money.'

'We're not talking about you.'

'All right, then. In answer to your question, no! Swanning in here once a year laden with expensive presents wouldn't do anything to improve this child's quality of life. You might think that that's the answer, but it isn't. In the end, it just disorients a child. I spent my childhood moving from pillar to post and it was upsetting. I know we're not talking about me, but my experiences are enough to tell me that what you're offering will be the same sort of thing. I won't have any child of mine subjected to that.'

'But why can't we stay in one place?' she could remember asking her mother. Over and over, until she realised that it was a futile question. She wasn't going to put up with her own child asking, 'Why can't Daddy be here with us like everyone else's?'

And anyway, long-distance relationships like that never lasted. They couldn't. After the initial burst of good intentions, things would begin to wane. The visits would become fewer and further between. They would be replaced by presents sent through the post at appropriate times, and then even those would inevitably dry up. It just wouldn't work out and it would be better if the whole thing did not begin.

And then, she thought, ashamed, there's the question of me, isn't there?

Angus Hamilton might find it easy enough to breeze into her life now and again because he was indifferent to her, but how was she going to feel? How would she ever be able to loosen the stranglehold that her love for him had on her, if she couldn't rely on his absence giving her the strength she needed?

She couldn't conceive how unsettling it would be, living in between his visits, desperately trying to break free but with the knowledge that he might appear, at any given moment, and send her hurtling back to square one. How would she ever begin to get her life back into order? It would be beyond her. Like Sisyphus pushing his rock up that hill only to find it slipping away from him before he could reach the top. Over and over again. A never-ending task of recurring pain.

'I have no intention of "swanning in here", as you call it, once a year, with presents to compensate for my not being around for the other three hundred and sixty-four days. I don't see that as accepting responsibility for my child any more than you do.' He stood up and went across to the window, which, prosaically, overlooked a small neat car park, and beyond that a tiny park hemmed in by row upon row of small, neat, doll's-house-type houses, all very tidy and characterless. 'No, that's not what I had in mind at all.'

'And what exactly did you have in mind?'

He didn't answer immediately. He stuck his hands into the pockets of his trousers and continued to stare outside, seemingly riveted by the lack of inspiring scenery.

His silence, for some odd reason, began to make her feel more nervous. She didn't like it. It was more ominous than his biting sarcasm and anger. What was he thinking? Had she thrown him? Had she put him in a spot with her flat refusal to accept money so that now he was forced to think on his feet and come up with an alternative? Was that it?

'I propose that we get married.' He slowly turned around so that he was facing her, and she stared at him in shock. After the first wild surge of colour, her face had gone white. 'You seem surprised,' he said laconically, moving away from the window to sit back down on the sofa.

'You must be joking.'

'It's not that surprising a proposition, is it?'

'Are you mad?'

'We get married and our child can grow up in a normal family environment. There won't be any part-time parenting, no lavish gifts to make up for unavoidable absences when I can't make a certain Saturday or a certain Wednesday afternoon. And it will have all the material advantages which I am in more than a good position to offer. You're right when you say that money doesn't make a good parent—or a happy child for that matter—but if the opportunity is there, then how can you sensibly deprive our child of it?'

'You're not listening to me!'

'You're alone in the world, Lisa. No family network that you can fall back on. Do you really feel comfortable with the thought of bringing up a baby with no support at all?'

'Of course it's frightening,' she answered unsteadily. 'I know it isn't going to be a bed of roses. I know there will be times when I wish there was someone there to take over, to help out, but...'

'But...?'

'But that's no reason to marry you. Can't you see that? There would be no love involved...' She dropped her eyes and stared down at her lap. 'Your lifestyle isn't suited to a family. It would be a terrible mistake.'

'Stop being naïve,' he said curtly, and she bristled at the note of command in his voice.

'I am not being naïve. I don't want to marry you.'

'I thought that marriage was high on your list of priorities,' he told her coolly, and she flushed. 'I thought that relationships with men were not to be contemplated unless a wedding ring was waiting just around the corner.'

'I never said that...'

'Of course you did. You just choose to forget.' He moved to where she was sitting and loomed over her, bending down so that the impact of his words wouldn't be lost across the distance of the room, so that she could feel his breath on her face. It brought back confusing memories of his body against hers, his fingers exploring her, his hands caressing her. She flinched at the unwanted images, averting her head, and his eyes narrowed.

'Do you regret what happened between us so much?' he asked, and although his voice wasn't raised there was no gentleness there. 'Do you now loathe me so much that you can't stand the thought of being in the same house as me?'

'It would be a mistake,' she repeated wearily, turning to look at him. 'It would be wrong. You say that marrying you would provide a normal life for our child, but it wouldn't, would it? What's normal about a marriage between two reluctant people, forced to live together for the sake of a child? What kind of environment would that be? A happy one?

'At least...' her voice had dropped to a whisper '...my parents loved each other. I might have hated all the travel, all the upheavals, but when I was inside the house with them, wherever that might have been, there was warmth and love there. What do you imagine it would be like without that?'

'I see,' he said, straightening up. He had removed his jacket earlier on. Now he slipped it back on and looked at her. 'I never imagined that I would find myself proposing marriage to a woman who would rather cope with a difficult situation in complete isolation than get tied up with me. What does that say about me, I wonder?' He laughed humourlessly.

'I'm sorry,' Lisa said.

'Don't apologise. Why should you?'

'It's just that I wouldn't want you to think that I don't consider your offer very generous...'

'But all in all the job just doesn't suit you.'

'That's it.'

'Which still leaves us with the problem of arranging some sort of visiting rights. And can we do that in an informal manner or would that not suit either?'

'We can work it out ourselves,' she replied, depressed because suddenly everything seemed to be not quite the right way up. After their heated confrontation, after his astounding proposal, his calm acceptance now was something of an anticlimax. Then she told herself that she was being utterly stupid. He would have to have access to their child, whether it disrupted her life or not, so wasn't it preferable that any such access was achieved with the least acrimony possible?

But at the back of her mind there was the niggling thought that he had surrendered awfully quickly once she had informed him that she wouldn't marry him. No protestations, no attempts to persuade her to change her mind. He must be relieved, she thought, with a stab of bitterness. Relieved that she had not taken him up on his offer, relieved that he had squared it with his conscience, had been seen in his own eyes to have done the right thing, so that now he could carry on with his life knowing that he had tried his best.

'Good,' he said abruptly. 'I'll be in touch.' And he turned away, letting himself out of the flat without a backward glance.

It was only when he had gone that she realised how drained she was. She switched on the television set and pretended to watch something but she was too fraught to concentrate.

Now that he had come and she knew that he would be back again, if only to sort out things, she was back on that tightrope of suspended animation. Doing normal things, like reading her book, washing the dirty mugs in the kitchen sink, carrying on except that her mind had been frozen in some dreadful time warp, dwelling obsessively on him, desperately looking forward to the next encounter. She would have to fight very hard if she wasn't to go through the next few months or years leaping from one emotional encounter to the next and only managing to exist in between.

If only she could do the sensible thing and dislike him. There were, after all, a million reasons why she should. If only, even, she could put him in some sort of perspective, but she couldn't. He overwhelmed her. Even when they were arguing, even when bitterness filled her mouth and her head and her thoughts, even when he alarmed her in a way no one ever had before, he still excited her. She found it hard to tear her gaze away from him, and when she did she could still see his face reflected in her mind.

On Monday, Paul, surprisingly because he normally respected her need for privacy, asked her about him. He didn't ask whether Angus was the man responsible for the pregnancy, but she told him anyway since there seemed little point in hiding it.

'And is he going to support the baby?' he asked casually. They were sitting in his office, going through the books, with a plate full of sandwiches between them and two cups of coffee. He was busy poring over the figures, frowning because his mind, which was so tuned in to anything to do with plants, found it almost impossible to piece together anything that involved numbers, and she hesitated, wondering whether to change the subject tactfully or not.

'He wants to contribute,' she said honestly. 'He wants to take some responsibility.'

'And you find that surprising?'

'No, not really,' she answered, thinking about it.

'In that case, why didn't you approach him from the start?'

'Because...' she said, faltering. He looked up at her

thoughtfully. 'Because I didn't want him to feel obliged to…'

'But he is; of course he is.' He was looking at her and his pleasant, open face was speculative. 'He struck me as a very aggressive type. The sort of man who wouldn't do anything in half-measures.'

'He has a very fast, very high-profile lifestyle. There's no room in it for anyone else.'

'And you resent that.'

'Of course I don't!' Lisa exclaimed.

'I don't mean to pry, Lisa,' he said a little tentatively, because her personal life was an area into which he had rarely ventured in the past, 'but if you were indifferent to him it wouldn't matter a jot to you whether you disturbed his lifestyle or not. Your only thoughts would be for the baby and you would probably find it easy to accept that he was duty-bound to share the responsibility.'

She didn't say anything. She knew what he was getting at but she couldn't put it into words; she couldn't come right out and admit that she was frantically in love with Angus Hamilton. To voice it would make it more real; it would be as though there was no turning back, no more hiding from the truth. She would have to don the public face of her private life, and, however much she had opened up with Paul recently, she still wasn't prepared to go that far.

'If you ever need somewhere to go,' he said, after a while, 'to think things over, the cottage is empty and you're welcome to it.'

He owned a two-bedroomed cottage in the Lake District. Lisa had been there once for a long weekend and she had rather enjoyed it, even though it was in a fairly sad state of repair, despite Ellie's brave attempts to hide it with new curtains and scatter cushions on the sofas. Paul had been given it by his father and apparently it had been in his family for years and years and years, and since each successive inheritor had done minimal work on it the task of now overhauling it would cost a fair penny.

She didn't think she would be needing to think anything over. She wouldn't need the cottage. There was, really, not much thinking over to be done. The fact was that Angus Hamilton would see his child and her only protection lay in her ability to forge ahead with her life and close her eyes to the effect he had on her. Time had a way of sorting things out, of putting things into focus.

'Thanks, Paul,' she said obediently, then she lowered her eyes and steered the subject back to work and he accepted the change without batting an eyelid. It was one of the things that she had liked about him from the very start. He had never allowed curiosity to dictate to him. He had left her to her privacy, the way she had liked it. Once. Sometimes, now, she wasn't entirely sure.

If she hadn't clung so tenaciously to her security, would she have been better prepared for the earthquake that had turned her tidy, ordered world upside down when Angus Hamilton had entered it? Brick by brick she had built the fortifications around her to protect her from life's slings and arrows, yet when he had come along it had taken only a puff to blow them all away.

If she had never tried to cling to the illusion that stability was somehow a controllable commodity, then wouldn't she have been less vulnerable in the end? Better prepared to cope with a man like Angus Hamilton? If, if, if. She could drown thinking about all the ifs in her life.

Still, she would have to learn to cope with her emotions, learn not to give herself away when she was with him, however infrequently that might be.

It was a week before she next saw him and this time when the doorbell rang she knew it was going to be him before she even got there. She composed her face suitably and opened the door, quite prepared to talk through the visiting rights issue in a dispassionate manner.

It was not quite seven and he had obviously come straight from work. He was still wearing his suit, which was dark grey, with his coat, which was black, and she looked at him politely, expecting him to get straight down to business, but when she invited him inside, in a voice which neither wavered nor stumbled, he asked instead whether she had eaten yet.

'I…was about to,' Lisa said hesitatingly.

'Get your coat. I'll take you out for a meal.'

'Why?' she asked, and he smiled at her with the speculative, amused charm that reminded her of how he used to be months ago on that holiday.

'That's not a very gracious response,' he murmured.

'I'm sorry, but I just thought that we might as well discuss whatever terms of visiting that you'd like right here. There's no need to take me out.'

'No, you're right, there's none, but the way I look at it is that we're going to be seeing one another on a regular basis for an indefinite length of time, even if it is only in passing. We might as well get accustomed to some sort of relaxed, amicable relationship.' He was still smiling, though the temperature in his voice had dropped by a few degrees. 'Or is that asking too much?'

'No, of course not.' He was right, and maybe a politely friendly arrangement was the way to go, after all. She smiled and said, 'I'll get my coat; I won't be a minute.'

They went to an Italian restaurant, which was lovely because she hadn't eaten out in a restaurant for ages, and over the meal he showed her photos of the Caribbean islands they had visited, which Liz had sent to him because, he explained, he never remembered to carry a camera anywhere.

'I think the problem,' he said lazily, 'is that the damn thing's just too complicated. It was my mother's. She used to take impressive shots of flowers. My problem is that I'm fairly useless when it comes to gadgets like that. Too many dials to twist.'

When he chatted like that, easily and without any of that cold cynicism which he was capable of, she could feel her guard dropping. She had to remind herself that charm was a commodity at his disposal, something he pulled out at will.

It was only when they were standing outside her flat that she said, with surprise, 'What about arrangements to see the baby? We haven't discussed it at all.'

'Oh, no, we haven't, have we?' he answered, as though startled himself by the omission. 'Perhaps I could call by next week and we can discuss it then. What about next Saturday?'

'I don't know,' Lisa said uncertainly. 'I'm not sure.'

'Why?' He looked at her with a slight frown. 'Are you going somewhere? We could make it another day if you'd prefer.'

'No.' Her face cleared. 'Saturday will be fine.' She decided that she was being foolish, that they had just spent a perfectly enjoyable evening together with no angry exchanges or bitter accusations.

'Right, then, I'll call for you around seven-thirty?'

She nodded, and watched him as he walked to his car, gave her a wave and then drove off.

She didn't quite know why but she felt unsettled by the evening. It didn't make any sense because when she sat down and thought about it she had nothing to feel unsettled *about*. He had been pleasant and charming in a totally unthreatening way. He had displayed the same polite, almost brotherly concern that he had shown towards her at the very start of that holiday, when he had been at pains to make her feel at ease.

It was a good thing, she told herself over the next few days, that they could relate to each other in a civil, adult fashion. What kind of life would it be for a child to be torn between two warring parents? And she would never be able to conduct her life in a state of constant emotional upheaval; she would end up having a nervous breakdown.

He had been angry and upset, she realised, when he had first found out about the pregnancy, but now he had had time to think things over and in his usual firm, calculating way he had taken the reins and was steering them in the most sensible direction.

He had offered marriage, but had not tried to fight her objections. No, he had wanted marriage as little as she had and now that that idea had been squashed he intended to conduct a courteous, occasional-dinners-out type of relationship with her so that when they met they would at least be able to exchange conversation without arguing.

She couldn't find fault with that, could she?

She was now nearly eight months pregnant. She didn't need to cope with unnecessary strain. Very shortly, she would be stopping work, and counting down the days on the calendar. She had already had a tour of the maternity section of the hospital where she would be having the baby, and it had had quite an impact on her. She needed to feel reasonably relaxed and it would help if she didn't have to do battle with a man whose presence was enough to throw her time and again.

So when she next saw him she was prepared to make an effort and she did.

They went out for a meal, this time at another restaurant where the music was a bit louder and the atmosphere a little more hectic, and when he asked her questions about what she had been doing for the past week she didn't frown and wonder whether there was anything more meaningful behind the questions; she just answered with a smile.

She told him that she only had a little over a week to go before she gave up working, but that she would be back again almost as soon as she'd had the baby because she needed the money, and it only occurred to her much later, when she was in bed, that he had not argued the point.

He had not informed her that she would have no need to return to work if she listened to him and accepted the money he wanted to give her. He had not pointed out that she had chosen not to marry him, that instead she had picked the harder of the paths to follow. There had been no recriminations and none of the terse, vaguely threatening accusations with which he had initially confronted her.

Instead he had nodded understandingly, moved on to discuss the maternity benefits in his company, which he was hoping to upgrade within the next year, while she ate and listened and was hardly aware of how fundamental his change in attitude towards her appeared to be.

Now, with the lights in her bedroom off, lying on her side with a pillow angled by her stomach, she realised that what was now missing between them was that spark which had manifested itself in passion when they had been on holiday and which had still glowed when they had argued heatedly over the fate of the baby.

They had reached some kind of even keel and she said to herself that nothing could be better. She even wondered whether her violent attraction towards him was beginning to ebb away. She had certainly relaxed enough in his company not to feel permanently on edge every time he looked at her. She could meet those blue eyes evenly and she had even stopped apologising in that automatic way of hers which appeared to have been a habit cultivated over a lifetime.

She also realised that they had discussed nothing practical, which had supposedly been the object of the exercise.

She decided that the next time she saw him she would insist that they reach some sort of agreement as to how often he would want to see the baby. She would do that before they went anywhere or did anything. She couldn't continue to see him as though they were friends.

She wouldn't allow herself to be lulled into some kind of false security. He didn't love her and he had nothing to lose, but she couldn't afford to become too dependent on his kind, solicitous visits because there would come a time when she would find that she couldn't do without them.

The next time she saw him, she would lay the cards on the table.

CHAPTER EIGHT

LISA had, stupidly, she now realised, left almost everything till the last minute. Her friends had given her bits and pieces over the months, which she had stored away in a cupboard, out of sight, but she had bought hardly anything herself. The cot, the pram, and all the other things which she vaguely assumed a baby might need, she had left to the very end.

At first, because she had not wanted to think about things like that, and anyway nine months seemed such a long time, she had kept telling herself that there would be more than enough time.

Later, when she had found herself unconsciously growing more and more attached to the baby inside her, she had held back because of some irrational fear of preempting fate by going out and buying things.

Then she had told herself that she would do it all when she gave up work, except that she had never really anticipated staying at work for quite as long as she had. Keeping busy had seemed so much more preferable to staying inside her house, day after day, preparing for the baby, being constantly reminded of how lonely it was going to be giving birth, then looking after a baby, all on her own.

The only thing she hadn't quite foreseen was how tired she would be in the latter stages of pregnancy.

But it's got to be done, she told herself after she had picked off some breakfast on the Saturday morning. The thought depressed her for no reason that she could put her finger on.

It wasn't as though she had no money in the bank because she had. She had been diligently saving every month. She could easily afford the cot and the pram and she hardly needed to buy any clothes at all because her friends had bought quite a few for her, though she hadn't looked at them for so long that she could hardly remember what exactly they were. All she could remember was holding them up, exclaiming with the right degree of pleasure in her voice, and then stuffing them away because the sight of them had made her feel like bursting into tears.

She cleared away her plate and cup slowly. Her pregnancy had been an easy one, with no complications. For the first few months she had felt sick occasionally, but then that had cleared and almost up until a couple of weeks ago she had felt perfectly fine.

Now it irritated her that she had to move so lethargically. Everything took three times longer than it normally would have. She never complained to anyone, though. She felt that she had no one to blame for getting herself in this situation and there was no way that she was going to moan about anything at all.

She brushed her hair, looked at herself in the mirror and decided that, all told, she didn't look too bad. Apart from her stomach, everything had remained more or less the same size.

She could remember Ellie telling her proudly that she had swollen to the size of a barrage balloon with each of her pregnancies, because she just couldn't stop eating and putting on weight.

Lisa's arms and legs had remained thin and her face looked healthy but that was all.

She sighed, gathered up her bag and slung it over her shoulder, then went to the front door and pulled it open.

Angus was standing outside and because she had had absolutely no warning that he would be there she very nearly yelped in shock.

'How long have you been here?' she asked. She hadn't spoken to him since she had made the decision to get this visiting business sorted out and to stop meandering into some kind of frightful, dangerous friendship with him.

She only wished that her body could be as pragmatic as her mind. She looked up at him and her heart fluttered at the dark sexiness of his face and the taut lines of his body.

It was cold and windy outside and the wind had tousled his dark hair, which somehow made him look less intimidating but rather more dangerous.

'I was about to ring the doorbell.'

'Oh.' Lisa stepped outside firmly and shut the door behind her. 'As you can see, I'm on my way out. I'm afraid you'll have to call back. It might be an idea if you phoned me in advance.' She hoped, with something approaching nausea, that his visiting times weren't going to be along these lines. Just showing up when it suited him and not giving her any advance warning. She had to brace herself for him. She didn't think that she could cope with surprise calls. She would have to make sure that he understood that when they discussed arrangements.

She began walking laboriously towards her car and he fell into step with her.

'Where are you going?' His questions never seemed to emerge as questions, she thought, more like politely phrased commands. All part and parcel of a man who had no time for uncertainties, who was accustomed to taking the lead and being followed.

'Shopping,' Lisa said, not looking at him. Her thick coat seemed to weigh ten times what it should and was pressing down on her, making her movements even more sluggish. The wind was blowing against her as well, so that it felt as though she had to do battle with it. At this rate she doubted that she would make it further than a few shops. 'There are some things I have to get,' she added vaguely.

'I'll come with you.'

He took her arm and steered her away from her car and towards his, which was a gleaming, high-powered anachronism among the other run-of-the-mill cars.

She tried to pull away and opened her mouth to tell him that she intended going on her own, but before she could say anything he told her, with silky authority in his voice, 'And don't even think of being stubborn and arguing with me. You've finally realised that you need to buy a few things for this baby, like something to sleep in, and I'm coming with you whether you want me there or not.'

'How did you know...?' she asked, blushing, surprised.

He said drily, 'I looked. No nursery. Nothing but a small spare room hastily cleared away and half-empty.'

'You nosed around my house!'

'Hardly. Your house is so small that I could sit in one spot and have a pretty good view of every room in it.'

He held the passenger door open for her and she settled herself inside, tucking her coat around her.

His appearance had thrown her. She now felt as though she had lost command over her own day but she was too stunned and taken aback to feel angry.

'Where to?' he asked, slipping in beside her.

She said stiffly, 'Reading, please. There are some children's shops there.'

'We'll go to Harrods,' he told her, and she bristled and twisted to face him.

'We will *not* go to Harrods! I can't afford anything from Harrods!'

'But I can,' he said smoothly. He drove off, heading out towards London.

'You can't take control like this,' she spluttered.

'Of course I can. We're going to Harrods and I shall be paying for whatever we get and there's no point in getting in a state over it.'

'You're impossible,' she muttered under her breath, staring out of the window and watching the built-up countryside of Berkshire give way to the busy network of roads leading into London.

After a while, he said, with a hint of amusement in his voice which made her even crosser, 'I can feel you simmering there next to me, ready to explode. Very bad for a woman in your condition. We don't want you going into premature labour, do we?'

'I'll make sure I spare you the experience,' Lisa snapped sarcastically, which left him unperturbed.

'I told you I intended taking responsibility. I have no idea why you're so surprised that I'm buying a few necessities for you.'

'Because I can buy them myself!'

'Now listen to me,' he said, with an edge of steel in his voice. 'I don't intend to go round in circles every time this business of money comes up. You just have to accept that I have a lot of it and I'm going to make sure that our child gets the best, whether you like it or not.'

She tried to think of something suitably cutting as a

rejoinder to this high-handedness, but she couldn't, so she lapsed into sulky silence until they were in Central London, when she said, sweetly, 'And where do you intend to park?'

He laughed, not looking at her. 'I don't.' He reached for his car phone, spoke into it and replaced the receiver. 'There. All done. George will meet us outside Harrods and take the car.' He flashed her a quick, sidelong glance, then returned his attention to the packed roads.

'How convenient, having a chauffeur at your beck and call,' she said under her breath.

'Isn't it?' He was smiling, and she shot him a look full of resentment. How was it that he could be so cheerfully immune to anything she had to say, when what she wanted most at the moment was to pick an argument with him?

She had come to the conclusion that if loving him was bad, then liking him was almost equally so, and she had caught herself doing both in the past few weeks. She would have to be frosty and polite and the only way she could achieve this would be to set him at a distance, to shift him out of this 'be kind to Lisa' approach which he appeared to have adopted recently. She didn't want him to be kind to her. She preferred his coldness to that.

George was faithfully waiting at the agreed spot for them, rubbing his gloved hands together, hurrying to the car as soon as it pulled over so that he could drive away with the least possible delay, and she allowed herself to be guided up to the Children's floor of Harrods, her body stiff with hostility.

If he noticed a thing, then he made no comment, just held her elbow and cleared a path through the crowds with seemingly very little effort.

'Now,' he said, 'where do we start?'

Lisa, who had perversely made up her mind to be as unhelpful as she could possibly get away with being, told him what she needed, and they proceeded to look at every cot, from every angle, until reluctantly she felt some of the coldness beginning to thaw.

She had had no idea that such a variety of cots existed. Some of them were works of art. She ran her hands along the smooth, dark wood and shyly began to relax.

He had told her that she was not to look at the prices of anything, had forbidden her to, but she still did and she flushed guiltily at the cost of some of the various bits they were looking at

From their joint positions of inexperience, they amicably discussed the merits of this or that over something else, and it was only after a while that she discovered she was enjoying herself, that this was the first time her eyes had been opened to what it must be like to be pregnant and involved with someone and that she liked it.

Why couldn't it have been different? she asked herself sadly. Why did I have to fall in love with a man as out of reach as Angus Hamilton? Why did I have to get pregnant? Why couldn't it have been Mr Ordinary from next door, so that we could have lived happily ever after like two people in a fairy tale? Why, why, why?

She looked up to find him watching her narrowly, and she forced herself to smile and carry on.

The cot they decided on wasn't the most expensive one, but it was getting there, and then they moved on to other things, other things which she had had no idea she might need, but which looked so wonderful, so tempting that she let herself be swayed by him, so that by lunchtime she was exhausted and uncomfortably aware that the money he had spent made her paltry savings look like bits of copper.

They had lunch at the café in Harrods, and she dabbled about with her sandwiches, so that he said wryly, 'I thought pregnant women were supposed to eat enough for two?'

Lisa laughed and looked at him briefly before lowering her eyes. It hurt too much to keep them on his dear face. It raised too many if onlys and whys in her mind, which made her feel tearful.

'Difficult when you're at this stage of the pregnancy,' she said, concentrating on another bite of sandwich. 'There's nowhere much for the food to go. I find it easier to pick.'

'And how's your conscience getting along?' he asked, pushing his plate aside and then leaning back in his chair to look at her. 'I watched you while we were up there, like a tiny little orphan who's suddenly found herself transported into the biggest toy shop in the world and can't quite believe that she's really there.'

'I'm not used to such extravagance,' Lisa told him with a small smile. 'I kept trying to tot up the cost of everything we were buying, but after a while my head couldn't hold such big sums and I had to give up.'

'I told you not to do that,' he drawled, but with amusement in his voice, and she felt the same pleasure she had felt earlier on when they had been looking at everything together—a feeling of absolute unity—so that she had to pull back and remind herself that any such feeling was an illusion.

'So you did,' she agreed, and he laughed and continued to look at her.

'Did you enjoy yourself?' he asked abruptly, sitting forward and resting his elbows on the table, his blue eyes intent on her face.

The place was humming with activity, people coming

and going, tables being cleared, but when he looked at her like that it was as if there was no one around them; it was as if the whole universe had narrowed down to just the two of them. She could feel her heart pounding.

'Did you?' he pressed softly, and she nodded and pushed her plate aside as well.

'It's easier with two, isn't it?' he asked her, though he didn't wait for a reply to a question which she would have found virtually unanswerable without giving herself away. 'Easier not having to cope on your own, easier not having to look at things which aren't meant to be looked at alone. Isn't it?'

This time he waited, his head tilted slightly to one side, his dark, powerful features revealing nothing.

'I don't suppose I would have browsed so much,' Lisa answered, hedging the question the best she could.

'Easier not to have complete and total responsibility on your own.'

'What are you trying to say, Angus?' she asked at last, raising troubled eyes to his 'It's always easier sharing responsibilities; of course it is. But sometimes it's just not possible.'

'Yes, it is.' His voice was low and urgent. 'Marry me, Lisa.'

She licked her lips and shifted in her chair. She felt like a rabbit which had been run to ground and was cornered. She was no longer even on her own home patch.

Was that why he had been so nice to her recently? Because he had been trying to warm her up to the thought of marrying him? But in a way that would not make her suspicious and have her running off in the opposite direction like a frightened deer?

She wished that she could explain to him how much

she would have wanted to marry him, but not like this, not under these circumstances. It was the cruellest of tricks that she should find herself with everything she wanted so nearly within her reach and yet so far.

'I can't,' she whispered, and he flushed darkly, with anger.

'Why not? Haven't I proved to you that we can co-exist? That I'm not some kind of monster?'

'I never said you were,' she protested. It was easy for him to speak of coexisting, she thought. From where he was sitting, she must appear stubborn and stupid, because as far as he was concerned they could rub along well enough together, well enough for their child to grow up in the presence of both parents, where a harmony of sorts existed.

If he could see deep into her mind, he would soon realise why any such situation was out of the question.

He would be able to give her the security of a house, with all the trappings, and that kind of security, she knew, was important. For a long time, she had thought that it was the only security she needed. But then she had met him and she had realised that there was a greater security than that. The security of being emotionally bonded to someone else, of having your love returned, of being anchored.

It had never occurred to her before, but in a blinding flash she could understand why her parents had never considered their nomadic lifestyle destabilising. Quite simply, it hadn't been. Their stability had lain in one another; it had transcended such things as geography. At night, they'd lain in one another's arms, and the fact that they were in a different bed, in a different house, in a different county had been immaterial.

'You're wasting your time, Angus,' she said, more

sharply than she might otherwise have done, and he brought his closed fist down hard on the table, so that the people sitting around them glanced across briefly, before looking away. 'And you can't threaten me or blackmail me or persuade me into seeing your point of view.'

'If you could give me just one good, coherent reason why you won't marry me, then I would understand,' he said harshly, in a low voice, leaning towards her so that his presence filled her head and made her feel a little dizzy.

'I already have!'

'You've told me that if we got married our child would grow up in an unhappy, inhibiting atmosphere. But when we're together, in case it's escaped you, you can enjoy yourself.'

'You don't understand.' He made it sound so easy. To make him understand seemed like a tortuous, uphill struggle. 'It's not as simple as that.'

'It's as simple or as complicated as you want to make it.'

'I don't know why you're so keen to...to get married,' Lisa said in a low voice. She had only made the observation with a view to buying time until she could work out some plausible line of defence, but when she looked at him she was surprised to see a dark flush of discomfiture cross his face, and vanish as quickly as it had appeared. Too quickly for her to try and work out what it meant, if anything.

'I mean,' she persevered, 'marriage and children were never part of your long-range plans.' Or maybe they were, she thought to herself, but just not with me. I was only ever good enough to fool around with. Isn't that how these upper-class types think? They might have their dalliances with any number of women but in the end they marry the ones who are suitable, whether or not love and attraction come into it.

Part of her told her that this didn't quite tie up with the Angus Hamilton that she knew, but then that was an emotional reaction to him.

'No,' he conceded abruptly.

'Well, then.'

'Well, then, what?'

'You can begin to understand how I must feel, Angus.' She took a deep breath and decided to lay as much of her hand on the table as she possibly could. 'We had a fling, not even an affair. A fling, for heaven's sake! Something that would have fizzled out after a few weeks under normal circumstances. Except that the un-expected happened. The unthinkable.' She lowered her eyes and stirred her now ice-cold coffee with the tea-spoon, swirling the liquid round and round so that it formed ripples like the surface of a dirty pond.

'Something that can't be ignored, or locked away in a cupboard somewhere,' he pointed out curtly, which kind of made her want to cry because they had had such a wonderful morning and she didn't want it all to end on a sour note.

'I know that. But marriage is going from one extreme to the other, isn't it?'

'It's a solution to a fairly extreme situation, wouldn't you say?'

'Do you want to marry me because you're an impor-tant person in an important, high-profile job and an il-legitimate baby would discredit you?' She looked at him evenly and saw something like the ghost of a smile cross his face.

'And where did that line of reasoning suddenly spring from?'

'Well...now that you mention it, Caroline...'

'Ah, yes, it had something of a Caroline ring about it,' he said grimly. 'Caroline lives her life playing to an audience. I don't. I really don't give a hang what the rest of the world thinks of me because I don't live my life for the rest of the world.'

'Then why...?'

'Because this is my child. I never considered marriage or a family, at least not in the foreseeable future. I also never considered what I would feel when fatherhood presented itself to me.'

She knew what he meant. Children, before, had been other people's problems. Now he looked at her, only a couple of weeks away from giving birth, to *his* child, and he wanted this child with a fierceness which he had never foreseen. That was why he didn't want to be a part-time father. That was why he wanted to marry her.

Chances were that even if she had continued their relationship, even if their relationship had stretched beyond a few weeks, he would never have married her because there would never have been a need to marry her. There was a need now, as far as he was concerned, except that *she* was playing only a secondary role in the whole proceedings.

'Yes, I see that, but...'

'But you can't have marriage without the trimmings. Without the declarations of love, without the magic and stardust.' His voice, when he spoke, was impatient and he made the whole concept of romantic dreams sound like the whimsical imaginings of a fool, which was probably how he saw them. 'Fine.' He looked straight at her. 'Marry me, Lisa. I love you.'

For just a second, time stood still. She had a second of intense, perfect happiness, then the bubble burst and reasoning reasserted itself and told her that those were empty words. They didn't mean a thing.

'I think we should go, Angus. I'm beginning to feel a little tired.'

He didn't say anything. He pulled his mobile phone out of his pocket, called George and then said that he would be there by the time they made their way down to the street.

He didn't mention another word about marriage until they were in the back seat of the car, when he turned to her and informed her that he was still waiting for her answer.

'I won't give up,' he said smoothly, when she didn't reply. 'I never give up on anything I want.'

'And you want this child.'

'That's right.' He folded his arms and she looked at his profile, clean and strong, with worried eyes.

She began to wonder why she was bothering to fight. Wasn't it going to be a losing battle? She had laid her cards on the table and so had he. He wanted her for the sake of his child and he was going to get what he wanted because he always did. Whether she liked it or not, he would insinuate himself into her life and erode her until she gave in.

'And what if you fall in love with someone else when we're married? What if I do?'

'You can't conduct your life based on some hypothetical speculation. What if this car goes over the edge of a cliff with us in it? What if the Third World War breaks out and the whole world goes up in smoke? When you start thinking like that, you can carry on ad infinitum.'

'Those things aren't likely to happen. It's far more likely that—'

'You'll marry me and then fall in love with another man, only to find yourself unhappily trapped in a situation of my making?' His voice was hard.

Lisa didn't answer. There was no possibility of that, she knew. The Third World War scenario was far more likely.

They had cleared the traffic of central London, and now they were picking up speed along the motorway. They would be back at her place in no time at all, and for the first time since he had voiced his preposterous suggestion that they get married she just wasn't sure. She just didn't know whether it *was* a preposterous suggestion. Hadn't they strolled through Harrods if not entwined like a loving couple anticipating the birth of their first child, then at least like friends, sharing a single dream?

And hadn't it been easier? She imagined what it would have been like trudging wearily through baby shops in Reading, choosing things happily enough but never escaping that edge of sadness, knowing that she should be sharing things like that with the father of her child.

She thought about all the months and years that lay ahead, the decisions that would have to be taken, the childhood illnesses that she would have to face on her own.

What, she thought a little desperately, am I to do? Which path do I go down? She could actually see her life in front of her. Her life was a wilderness and the paths forked in opposite directions.

So, he didn't love her. Well, he must at least *like* her. He surely wouldn't have proposed if he hated her, would he? She might not be his first choice as a partner for life, she might not even be his second or third, but, as he'd said, these were exceptional circumstances.

And would it be so awful? She had so much love in her heart—enough for the two of them. And maybe one day, when he was least expecting it, he might turn around and realise that he did in fact love her, that time had nourished something which didn't presently exist into fruition.

'And what if *you* stray?' she asked timidly.

'Then you can divorce me and have full custody of our child and I'll abide by whatever rules you want.'

'I never imagined…that things would turn out like this for me.'

'You imagined that you had learnt lessons from your childhood and that you could arrange your life in such a way that it fitted in with what you wanted?'

'Yes.' Except now it was difficult to remember what those lessons were. Falling in love with Angus Hamilton had turned those preconceived ideas on their head and whenever she tried to grasp the things that had kept her going all this time she found that they were not quite within her reach.

'I know I'm not your type…'

'You know less than you think,' he answered ambiguously.

'I'm not a social butterfly. I'm no good at arranging dinners for twenty. I don't glitter and sparkle.' She knew that she sounded as though she was apologising, but she couldn't help it.

They had reached the outskirts of Reading now. Angus pressed a button so that the glass partition separating them from George in front slid aside, and he gave brief directions to the driver, then leaned back in his seat and looked at her.

'Will you let me think about it?' she asked, and he nodded. 'I'll call you.'

'No. I'll call *you*.'

'Don't you trust me?' she enquired with a faint smile, which he returned.

'Not when it comes to this. I'll drop by on Wednesday.'

The car pulled up outside her flat and now that they had arrived she felt a desperate urge to get inside, where she could be alone with her thoughts and decide for herself what she should do, without Angus's handsome, clever face swaying her every thought.

'Yes, OK.'

She pushed open the car door and Angus got out and said wryly, 'The bags in the boot?'

'Oh, yes, right.' She had forgotten about those. The big items were due to be delivered on Monday, but they had also bought an assortment of smaller things which had, in the mood of the moment, fallen into the category of cute, unnecessary and utterly irresistible.

He helped her with them into the flat, deposited them on the sofa, and before he left he turned to her and said, 'No more wriggling, Lisa.' He looked at her for a long time, then he did something completely unexpected. He reached out and laid both his hands on her stomach, caressing it, and she felt a spring of desire gush into life.

'No,' she agreed faintly, her body tensing, against her will, in expectation of his hands sliding upwards to her breasts. They didn't. He let them fall to his sides then turned around and let himself out of the flat.

She went across to the window, from where she could see his car, and watched as he slid into the back seat, leaning forward to say something to George, and she continued watching until she could no longer see it. Even after it had disappeared, she remained by the window and imagined the car heading back towards London, towards his place. Where was it? What was it like? There was so much, she realised, that she didn't know.

Then she spent the afternoon, and the rest of the week-end, unpacking all the assorted bits and pieces which she had collected over the months.

On Monday morning, she telephoned Paul as soon as she got up and asked him whether his offer of the loan of the cottage was still on.

'Isn't it too far for you to travel,' he asked dubiously, 'in your condition?'

'I'd really like it, Paul. I need to sort myself out; I need to get away from the house, just for a couple of days.' She didn't really know whether it would help being in a different place, but she thought that it might. She might be able to think clearly and lucidly without her familiar walls around her, and the familiar sights of those baby things lurking in the spare room, waiting in readiness as time ticked by and the day that had seemed so far away crawled nearer and nearer.

'It'll be cold. It'll take a little while to warm up.'

'No matter. I shall be back by Wednesday afternoon.'

She could sense him thinking, worrying about her, but he finally said that she could. He said he would make sure that Ellie stayed in so that she could get the key, and that he would also have her prepare some food—no arguments, please, or else no cottage—which made Lisa smile.

At a little after ten, after she had thrown a few things together in her case, she dropped by his house and collected the key along with enough food to last the duration of her stay and waged a friendly war with Ellie about the sanity of going somewhere so far when the baby was just around the corner and she should, really, be putting her feet up and taking it easy.

'I'll take it very easy,' Lisa promised. 'As soon as I get there. Feet up and all that stuff. And I won't have to cook. Thank you so much, Ellie.' But when she looked in the rear-view mirror as she drove off she could still see Ellie's face as she stood on the pavement outside their house, looking concerned and worried.

It was going to be a long drive, but at the end of it she would find peace—peace in which to decide what she should do with her life.

And, she thought, it was a fine day for driving. Cold and clear and blue. A good day to start a trip, as her father used to say every time they left one place and headed towards another. A good day to make the biggest decision of her life.

Look at me, Mum and Dad, she said to herself, no more that frightened little thing. Wherever you are, I know you'd be proud! She smiled.

CHAPTER NINE

IT WAS a good drive up. Lisa stopped at every service station she passed, so that she could stretch her legs, and she switched on her stereo for the entire drive. The various disc jockeys' voices boomed through the small car and it felt as though she had company.

Halfway through the journey, she pulled off the motorway, took a side road, parked the car in a lay-by and ate some of the sandwiches which Ellie had prepared. They tasted wonderful. She could already feel her head getting clearer. As she put distance between her and her house, the cobwebs began falling away and quite a bit of that worried agonising which she had done the previous night, alone in bed, began to recede.

By half past three, she was at the cottage. It was just as she remembered it. Small, clean, with minimum mod cons. A typical holiday home, Paul was always telling her, begging for attention except that no one could be bothered because it was never used enough to warrant a great deal of money being spent on it.

The ground floor was all open-plan, with the sitting room flowing into the kitchen, separated from it only by the width of a counter.

In the sitting room, there was a large, open fireplace and a stack of logs next to it, neatly contained in a basket which had seen better days but which comfortably matched the rest of the place.

Before she even unpacked, Lisa switched on the central heating, which cranked into life. It had been a fairly mild winter so far, so although it was very cold in the cottage there wasn't that deep-frozen feeling which tended to attack unused places in the depths of winter.

By the time she had hauled her bag upstairs and unpacked her few possessions, then laid out the food in the kitchen, it had warmed up enough for her to remove her coat, and, an hour later, her thick cardigan.

Ellie had prepared a generous hamper of milk, eggs, bread, several cans of several things, coffee, juice, butter—everything that Lisa could possibly need—and she made a mental note to buy her a huge bunch of flowers on the way back.

It was already dark by the time five o'clock rolled round—dark and warm and cosy—and she settled onto the sofa with her feet up and lay there with a cushion behind her head and her hand on her stomach and let herself think.

Her mind drifted into the past. She remembered bits of her childhood days, happy memories that filled the cottage like warm companions.

She remembered how she had longed for a life of security, but here, with no sounds around, just the silence of the darkness outside pressing against the windowpanes, she couldn't recapture the passion with which she had longed for it.

Fate had thrown her into an impossible situation where that placid, settled contentment which she had envisaged for herself would simply never materialise. Fate had thrown her Angus Hamilton and now, because she already knew what her decision was going to be, she began to enumerate the reasons why marrying him was what she intended to do, why it was the right thing to do, the only thing, in many ways.

It wasn't, she argued to herself, as if she could turn her back on him and walk away. It wasn't as though she could ever find again any sort of happiness in the monotonous tenor of her life. Even if she never laid eyes on him again, which was out of the question because of this child inside her, things would never be the same. He had filled her with the sort of wild, uncontainable passion that made a mockery of everything that was ordered and neat and safe.

It was as though she had lived her life like a two-dimensional cardboard cut-out, and he had taken her and given her shape and form, made her into a three-dimensional human being, with all the attendant problems.

And that, she knew, was her greatest problem. Whatever lay before her, she would never again be that cardboard cut-out. He had changed her and she would remain changed until the day she died, whether he stayed as a part of her life or not.

I can't be wary any more, she thought to herself. I have to meet this challenge even if it leaves me broken in the end.

And anyway, maybe it wouldn't. Hope would give her the impetus to carry on and who knew? Who could see into the future? She might get to like dinner parties for twenty. She might just find that it wasn't as bad as she'd imagined. She might find that laughter came easily after a while. She might well discover that she could shed the defensive caution that had sat on her shoulders from as far back as she could remember.

In a strange way, he had made her into the sort of

person she had never thought she could be. She had discovered deep within her some spark of impulse, some stirring of recklessness, something of her parents, and nothing had extinguished it and nothing, she now knew, ever would.

Later, at a little after seven, she made herself some food, opening one of the cans which Ellie had thoughtfully provided and helping herself to some pasta which was already in the cottage. Basic provisions, Ellie had told her, were always kept in the cupboards because they did use the place at least once every five weeks or so and they planned it so that they only had to bring perishables with them when they came to stay.

Then she settled down to read her book. There was no television. They had been adamant about not having one installed, despite pleas from the children, because they'd decided that there was already too much television at their house without it taking over their lives at the cottage as well.

Lisa didn't miss it. In the car, it had been fine listening to the voices talking at her out of the radio, but here it would have been intrusive.

It was only when she found herself drifting into sleep that she went upstairs, had a bath and then settled into bed.

There were only three small bedrooms in the cottage, but they were very pretty bedrooms, oddly shaped with sloping roofs. This one had a skylight and from where she lay she could look up and see the black, starry sky. She fell asleep thinking that out there, in another part of the country, the same black, starry sky was looking down on Angus, wherever he was. Working probably. It wasn't yet eight-thirty. Would he stop working such long hours when she married him? When he had this baby to come home to?

When she next woke up, it was black and silent outside and she had a brief moment of woolly disorientation which threw her into a panic as she wondered where she was. Then, sleepily, she remembered, and closed her eyes and felt it. The twinge that had awakened her, a cramping feeling. A contraction.

Oh, no—oh, my God, no! she thought. In real panic, she reached out to switch on the bedside lamp and in the process sent her alarm clock skittering across the darkened room. The noise, intruding into the silence, was piercing and nerve-racking.

She lumbered out of bed, her movements clumsy, and another contraction made her bend over double, grunting with pain. The blackness and the isolation, which had been comforting earlier on, were now a hostile force that brought home the seriousness of her situation in a way that nothing else could.

She was in labour, much earlier than her expected date, and contrary to what her doctor had confidently told her at her last antenatal appointment three days previously. At that point the baby had not yet engaged and he'd predicted that it would be late. Very few babies were born on their due date, he had told her. Some arrived early but most arrived late and he had assured her that she fell into the latter category.

She headed for the stairs, very slowly, and she was trembling by the time she made it to the telephone.

When she picked up the receiver and heard nothing at the end of it, she began to shake. She felt ill and lost and terrified.

She hadn't even bothered to check to make sure that

the phone was working when she had arrived. She had just assumed that it would be. She had assumed that Paul and Ellie would have known if it had been disconnected for whatever reason.

Another contraction and now the dreadful pump of adrenaline through her made her act quickly, switching on lights to ward off the frightful darkness, hunting for her bag containing her car keys, which she located just when she had more or less given up in desperation.

She slung her coat on over her nightdress, made it to the car, and had actually driven it partially down the track, with the trees pressing down on either side, when she realised, with horror, that she wouldn't be able to go the distance. She wouldn't even be able to make it to the main road, never mind that she had no idea where the hospital was even if she did. The contractions were coming stronger and harder, making her grit her teeth together in pain, turning her stomach into a hard rock that made her cry out.

She couldn't even begin to think of what she could do next. The pain made thinking too difficult. She switched off the engine, made her way to the back seat, and she had no idea how long she had lain there, with the pain getting more and more unbearable, when she heard the roar of a car and the screech of brakes as it scudded to a halt behind her.

She didn't care who the hell it was. It was help. She didn't care whether it was a car-load of robbers on their way to ransack the cottage. By God, she would collar them and make them take her to the hospital, or at least to the nearest house where she could use a phone and call for help.

Her eyes were squeezed shut and in between her cries

of agony she was panting. She heard the door being yanked open and then a muttered exclamation before someone reached inside the car and she felt herself being lifted out.

She opened her eyes and saw, in a haze, that it was Angus. Carrying her to the house, opening the door with her key and then kicking it wide open.

'How long?' he demanded, putting her down on the sofa, and she tried to answer but only a long groan emerged. 'Have you telephoned the ambulance?'

'Not working,' Lisa panted. The sweat had cooled on her. She felt slippery and incoherent.

'Dammit! Don't move. I'll be back.'

'Don't move'? Where did he imagine that she was going to move *to*? Did he think that she might go for a quick jog through the woods? Or lumber towards the kitchen to politely fix him a cup of coffee?

It occurred to her that she didn't have any idea what he was doing here, at the cottage, and it also occurred to her that she didn't care. His presence had taken the sharp edge off her terror, though not the tremendous pain. That was still there and getting worse.

She had been to her antenatal classes, and they had all sat around in a civilised group discussing pain-killers. What a joke! To think that she was here now and the only pain-killer in sight was the cushion, which she was biting hard on for all her worth.

'The ambulance is on its way. I've called them from my car phone.' She heard his voice from a long way off and raised her frightened eyes to his, while he stroked her hair back from her forehead and reached out to take her hand in his.

'My darling,' he whispered. 'Hold on. They won't be

long. Hold on, my darling. Half an hour at the outside. This place is in the middle of nowhere.'

Had he called her *darling*? She couldn't think. She could hardly breathe and she could hear the high sounds of her cries, torn out of her body, wild and primitive. She squeezed his hand tighter.

'Angus, I've decided...'

'Not now.'

'Angus...!'

'Later, my love, later.'

'Listen to me!' she yelled at the top of her voice. 'The baby! The baby's coming.'

And then things started happening with such speed that she forgot where she was, even forgot *who* she was. She wondered whether he was feeling the same numbing terror that was spreading through her, but when she looked at him as he laid her on the rug in front of the fire he was calm, a deep, reassuring calm that was as soothing on her nerves as any pain-killer could have been.

His voice, ebbing and falling continually, was deep and comforting.

How could she ever have wondered, at those antenatal classes, how she would know that she had gone into labour?

Then her mind went completely blank and nature took over. A strong, driving force that made her body do what it should, when it should. She heard Angus say, 'You're doing beautifully, darling.' Then, almost on top of that, he said, with an emotion that made his voice break and which was as primitive as any emotion she herself had felt, 'I can see the head.'

And the baby was delivered just as the ambulance

wailed up to the cottage, sirens going, people every-where. Lisa's eyes met Angus's, the question formed on her lips, and he answered it before it could be asked.

'We have a girl.'

They were bundled into the ambulance and driven with immense speed along the deserted roads towards the hospital, with Angus pelting along behind them in his car. They had wrapped the baby in a cream-coloured blanket and Lisa stared at her for the duration of the drive.

She couldn't believe it. She had to keep stroking the tiny head with its mass of dark hair; she wanted to smother the little, crumpled face with a million kisses. She wanted to collapse with happiness. She couldn't even remember the pain and terror. That all seemed like a long time ago.

'We'll have to take her from you,' one of the uni-formed men said, bending over her. 'Just for a short while!' He held up his hand, smiling at the protest that was already forming on her lips. 'To check her over, make sure that everything's all right. It's not every day that we arrive to find that the baby's already been deliv-ered.'

She nodded obediently, then there was yet more ac-tivity as they got to the hospital, and lots of smiling faces and 'Well done's' from seemingly everyone they bumped into.

She was carried in on a stretcher and was told that she would have to be thoroughly checked over, to make sure that everything was in order, and she nodded obedi-ently again.

'We won't be long with you, my dear,' the doctor said—another smiling face. They were all making her feel like a national heroine instead of a complete idiot who had done the most foolish thing in the world by going to stay in that cottage in the middle of nowhere when her baby was imminent.

She wondered, for the millionth time, where Angus was. Now that she could actually think, she wondered whether she had imagined those words of endearment back at the cottage.

'Where's Angus?' she asked.

'Is that your young man? Outside. He wanted to come with you in the ambulance, but there wasn't enough room. He can come in as soon as I'm finished with you.'

During the brief but thorough examination, the doctor made complimentary, slightly awestruck remarks about Angus's coolness, his capability.

'Seemed far less nervous than I was when I delivered my first baby!'

Then, at long last, he left her alone, and when Angus walked in she felt just as shy and tongue-tied at his presence as she had felt all those many, many months ago, when he had walked into a different hospital room to see her after her accident.

He was as dishevelled as she had ever seen him. His hair looked as though he had raked his fingers through it several hundred times and there was darkish stubble on his face. And she didn't know what to say. She just knew that she adored this man, no matter whether the feeling was returned or not.

'You look as though you've had a rough night,' she said weakly, lying back on the pillows, and he pulled a chair over to the bed and sat next to her.

'I have had a rough night, now that you mention it. I'll tell you about it some time. How are you feeling?'

'Wonderful,' she answered truthfully. 'On cloud nine, as a matter of fact. They've taken her away to do a few tests, just make sure that everything's where it should be.'

'I know. I saw her.' He looked a little overwhelmed. 'And now that I've got you to myself there are just one or two things that I want to ask you.'

'You're going to ask me why I went up there.'

'Why did you?'

'I needed to think. I had no idea that I would end up doing more than thinking.' She couldn't seem to stop herself from grinning. She wanted so much to tell him how much she loved him, and it was only the thought of seeing him turn away, unable to reciprocate the emotion, that made her hold back.

She didn't want this one day to be marred by anything. It was the most wonderful day of her whole life and she wanted to keep it that way.

'How on earth did you find me?' she asked.

'I got a phone call from Harrods.'

'Harrods?' She frowned, puzzled, and he shook his head woefully, as though he was talking to something not quite all there.

'You remember that large department store where we went to buy a few bits and pieces? They tried to deliver the furniture to you and there was no reply, so they telephoned me at work. I knew that something didn't quite make sense because you had been quite sure that you would be at your house, ready and waiting for them when they called. So I telephoned your boss, because, quite frankly, he was the only person I could think of.'

'And Paul told you.' She nodded.

'I needn't tell you that I let him have an earful for

sending you on your way to that cottage in your condition. I dropped what I was doing and headed up here immediately.'

'Oh, dear.' Lisa giggled and reddened. 'I'm glad you came, though.' She paused and then said in a rush, 'I can't begin to thank you enough. I don't know what I would have done—' Her thoughts were interrupted by a knock on the door, which as a gesture of politeness was hardly worth it, because a nurse entered almost immediately with a transparent carry-cot which she mounted by the bed, and another nurse followed with the baby. Her baby. *Their baby.*

She was absolutely perfect, the senior nurse told them, which Lisa thought was a little irrelevant since she could have told them that herself; she weighed a little over seven pounds and she could sleep for another hour or so, but then would need a feed. Lisa was to call if help was needed. The nurse then offered her congratulations to both of them, adding, 'Won't this be one to tell the grandchildren?'

Then both nurses left and Lisa and Angus stared at the baby. When she looked at him, she saw, with a burst of pride and elation, that he was looking at the little over seven pounds scrap of humanity as though he had never seen a baby in his life before.

Let me savour this moment of perfection for just a little longer, Lisa thought to herself. She decided not to mention anything about marriage just yet because that would be like coming back to earth with a bump. She had already relegated his whispers of tenderness to the realms of imagination induced by circumstance. Her mind must have been playing tricks on her because, although he was being kind enough now, there certainly hadn't been any repetition of 'darling' or anything of the sort.

So she said, looking at the sleeping baby in the cot, 'She's still an "it". We must think of a name.'

'What do you like?' He was still looking at the baby, couldn't take his eyes off her.

Lisa thought and said finally, 'Emily. Emily was my mother's name.' And this baby, she thought, is going to be free like my mother was, free from all those hang-ups that plagued me, free and happy and secure, what-ever her surroundings. She's never going to be scared of taking life into both her hands and living it to the fullest.

'Emily Natasha.'

'Why Natasha?'

'My grandmother's name.'

Which was lovely, Lisa thought, and just left the sur-name.

'Angus,' she said hesitantly, 'I know we're going to have to discuss this, so we might as well do it now. The reason I went up to Paul and Ellie's cottage, like I said, was to think. I had to get away and I had to get myself sorted out.'

He didn't say anything. Just strolled across to the win-dow and stared out, and she wished that he had remained back where he had been, instead of moving away, put-ting a barrier between them.

'I've been so confused. I can't begin to tell you what it was like when I found out that I was pregnant.' She looked down at Emily, Emily Natasha, lying in the hos-pital cot, on her back with both her arms stretched above her, her fists tightly closed, her legs bent at the knees. She couldn't believe that this beautiful creature had started its life as an unwanted pregnancy.

Angus was looking at her in silence, a silence which was neither encouraging nor off-putting, merely waiting to hear whatever she had to say. What was she going to tell him? Enough, she thought, but not too much.

'I was so shocked and horrified and lost I felt as though I had suddenly found myself trapped in a box, with nowhere to turn and no one to turn to.'

'You could have done the most obvious thing and turned to me,' he said roughly, and she smiled.

'But I couldn't, could I?' she asked sadly. 'We hardly knew each other.'

'Some would say that we knew each other very well.'

'When I thought of you, all I could see was an immense gulf, with me on one side and you on the other side. I'm not a fool, Angus. I might not have all the polish and finesse of the other women you've been out with, but I'm not a fool. I know that when we slept together all we were doing was giving in to impulse.'

She laughed to herself. How strange to think that she had once been an inhibited creature. Impulse was something that she'd associated with unhappiness. She'd never known that she would discover it was also what made the vital difference between living and existing.

'I never expected anything to come of our...' She sighed. I never expected it, she thought, but, like a fool, I hoped. 'I always knew that we were too different for anything between us to last.' She risked a glance at him but his face was unreadable and she dropped her eyes, back to the sleeping miracle in the cot.

'You ran away,' Angus said, without any hint of accusation in his voice, merely stating a fact, and she nodded.

'Yes, I ran away. I ran away because you invited me

to become your mistress and all I could see was an invitation to be hurt because it would be a relationship with no conclusion.' She waited a bit to see whether he would dispute that, and when he didn't she swallowed down the lump of regret and carried on. 'Then I found out that I was carrying your child. I know you think that I should have told you, but I couldn't. I knew what kind of life you led. I knew that if I turned up on your doorstep and dropped this bombshell on you your life would be wrecked.'

He didn't answer but a look of dark impatience crossed his face.

'Of course, I hadn't banked on bumping into Caroline.'

'Who informed you in no uncertain terms, just as she had on the yacht, no doubt, that whatever you thought you were spot on.'

'I didn't need Caroline to support my views,' she told him with heat in her voice, but then she looked back down at Emily and felt calm and in control again. 'I would have arrived at the same conclusions with or without her. No, I bumped into Caroline and I knew that it would get back to you that I was pregnant.'

Another accident of fate, she thought. Ever since she had met him, she had been destined to have accidents of this nature, or so it appeared.

'And when you asked me to marry you...'

'It was your worst nightmare come true.' He strolled across to the bed and perched on the side of it.

'How do you imagine a woman feels when she's proposed to by a man out of a sense of obligation?' She wanted to dislike him when she said this, but she found that she couldn't. She wondered whether she really ever had. Maybe a little voice in her head had told her that she needed to dislike him, and she had listened to that little voice and assumed that it was how she felt. 'I always imagined that a proposal of marriage would be a wonderfully romantic moment…'

She found that she couldn't continue because her eyes were filling up with tears and her voice was beginning to waver. She had to make an effort to go on.

'My father proposed to my mother on bended knee. She told me. They were only eighteen at the time, and then they waited until he'd finished his university course before they got married. When he proposed, he gave her a bunch of flowers, then he spent half an hour discussing the leaves…can you believe that? Mum said that she was enchanted.'

'It certainly sounds like a magical moment,' Angus said drily, which made her laugh a bit. 'How did they die?'

'In a car accident.'

It was something that she had never talked about. At the time, there had been no one close enough to her in whom she could confide, and then, later, she had not wanted to; she'd preferred to keep their memory stored away inside her, carefully preserved like the pressed flowers she used to collect as a child.

'They were going into town to get some stuff—food—preparing for yet another leap into the unknown. I was at home, studying madly. It was very rainy and there was a collision with a lorry that lost control and swerved across the central reservation. They both died instantly.'

She took a deep breath. 'The fact is, my parents were a romantic couple, and although I don't think I ever appreciated that at the time, something must have embedded itself in my head, because I always assumed that I would find romance. Instead what I found was a fling with a man and a baby on the way.'

It could have been romantic, she thought; it could have been everything she'd ever wanted and more, except that romance had to involve both people and there was no love from him, and, whatever hopes she'd had, she had to face the fact that there probably never would be.

'Anyway, I don't suppose any of this is relevant. I just wanted you to know the reasons why I had to think very hard about this marriage thing.'

There was movement in the cot and Emily's eyelids began to flicker and then her eyes opened. Blue eyes. She had Angus's bright blue eyes and his dark hair. Lisa instantly pressed the buzzer for the nurse.

She needs feeding, she thought, panic-stricken. What do I do? What if I drop her?

She was relieved, though, that there was this intrusion, because the conversation had been so intense, and she was very much afraid that if she had carried on much longer she would have ended up telling him everything, telling him how she felt.

She would never tell him how she felt. She had made that decision. She would marry him but she would never trap him in a situation where he felt constrained by the fact that she loved him and he didn't return the love.

The nurse bustled in as she was lifting Emily out of the cot, and Lisa looked at Angus, embarrassingly aware that she was about to breast-feed and willing him to go away, but he didn't move. He remained sitting where he was, and she felt her face growing redder and hotter as the baby fumbled by her nipple before finding it and beginning to suck.

He is the father, she thought, but when she raised her eyes to him she still felt hot.

'And...?' he asked.

'And my answer is yes.' She looked down at the tiny thing at her breast and prayed that she had made the right decision.

CHAPTER TEN

LISA didn't quite know what she had expected Angus to say. It was a scenario which she hadn't worked out in her mind. What she hadn't expected was the complete lack of response. Total silence. And she didn't dare lift her eyes to meet his because now a dreadful uneasiness began to sweep over her.

What if he had changed his mind? She concentrated very hard on Emily's mouth, working vigorously at her breast. A strong feeder, the nurse had said, despite being a little early.

All the while, she was wondering why he hadn't said a word. Perhaps the reality of a child had only now sunk in. It worked that way with some people. They imagined parenthood as a cosy little picture with a forever smiling child who never screamed its head off and went to bed when it was told.

Had delivering his own baby opened his eyes to how much his life would change if she married him and he found himself a husband and father? She had thought that it had been an intensely emotional moment for him, and perhaps it had been, but maybe now that that brief excitement was over he was already thinking ahead and not liking the look of what he was seeing.

Was that it?

Her hair hung down across her face, shielding her from eyes which she didn't want to meet, eyes that would gently tell her that he had changed his mind, that she had her freedom. Eyes that wouldn't see the bald truth, which was that she no longer wanted her freedom. It was a commodity which was no longer hers to enjoy, not if he wasn't around.

She had thought, when he had first proposed to her, that to accept would be to condemn herself to a prison in which she lived with the man she adored, but was forever trapped in the hopeless situation of one whose love was not returned.

She realised now that the real prison would be her flat in Reading, her job at the garden centre and a life without focus. The misery of living with him would be infinitely preferable to the misery of living without him.

She had so resigned herself to what she assumed was going through his head that she finally said, breaking the silence between them, 'Of course, if you've changed your mind...then it's not a problem.' She looked at him. 'We can easily work out arrangements.' Emily appeared to be dropping back off to sleep and she removed her from her comfortable position at the breast, drew her robe together, and held her over her shoulder, supporting her with both her hands.

'I—I'm sorry,' she stammered. 'I've been a bit silly. I never thought that you might change your mind. I...'

'I haven't.'

Lisa looked at him, confused. 'Then you still want me to marry you?'

Emily had fallen asleep. Lisa could tell from the slow, rhythmic breathing and she gently lowered her back into the cot and then folded her arms.

'Will you tell me why *you* changed your mind?'

Because I just can't live without you.

'I just thought it over. I realised that it was the most practical thing to do.'

'And what about love?'

'As you said, a successful marriage… Lots of people have stars in their eyes when they get married, and then everything goes wrong… This is more of an arrangement, I know…'

Why did she feel so unhappy? she wondered. Was it because all this talk about arrangements and practicalities was such an anticlimax after Emily's arrival? She told herself that Emily's birth had transported her to another planet, a planet where worries couldn't intrude, but now she was back down to earth and what else could she expect?

How could I ever have thought myself to be a sensible, controlled person? she thought. I'm little more than a hopelessly romantic, incurably impulsive fool.

Angus moved closer to her, sitting so near now that she could have touched his thigh with her hand.

'There are certain conditions,' he began. 'I'm not sure that you'll find them at all acceptable.'

She was feeling more unhappy by the minute. She wondered whether it could be a symptom of postnatal depression. They had spent an entire class devoted to postnatal depression. Maybe that was why she was feeling so tearful. She wished that he hadn't mentioned conditions. That was so cold and clinical. Would he want her to sign something as well? Some legally drawn up contract laying out the terms of their marriage, like a job contract?

She smiled bravely and said, 'Of course, I understand. I know I shall be expected to mingle with your friends. I'm not used to things like that, cocktail parties and business dinners, but I know that that will be a condition of my marrying you. I hope I won't let you down. I hope I won't prove to be an embarrassment.'

She stopped talking. Something had crossed her mind. What if, by 'conditions', he meant that he should be allowed to have affairs outside marriage? She hadn't thought of that before but she was no great beauty and he mixed in a world of glamorous, tempting women, women for whom married men were not out of bounds, but fair prey. A solitary tear trickled down her cheek and she hurriedly brushed it away.

'Of course, I'm not a great cook. I may have to take lessons...' She didn't want to think about other women in his life. She didn't want to think of him loving anyone or making love to anyone.

'You silly little fool...' he said, catching her hands in his.

'I know,' Lisa said in a small voice. 'I know I'm not very sophisticated. I realise that—'

'Stop talking and listen to me.'

Except he didn't say anything, which made her think that he was trying to work out in his mind how to phrase what he wanted to say, what he *needed* to say, trying to find the right words to tell her that he could never love her, that he was no longer even attracted to her, that she would merely be around because of his daughter.

'I'm not sure how to say this...' he began, and she took a deep, calming breath and braced herself. 'I haven't got many conditions, but they're important ones, and if you don't feel that you can meet them, then you're free, Lisa. Condition number one is that you give up your job at the garden centre.'

'Of course.'

'We could live in London, but only until we find somewhere out in the country. I don't want my daughter being brought up in London. London is no place to raise a child.'

'No,' she said.

'We can start looking for somewhere just as soon as you feel able to. It will have to be within commuting distance of London. Condition number two is that...' He paused and she waited for the bomb to detonate. 'Condition number two is that you start trying to like me.'

'I do like you, Angus.'

'No.' He shook his head and tilted her chin up with his finger. 'No, I mean... I never thought that I would say this to anyone; I never thought that I would have to... Friendship is all well and good... The fact of the matter is...'

A long silence followed and eventually she said, 'What is the fact of the matter?'

Angus sighed heavily and raked his fingers through his already tousled hair. Did he know what an endearing gesture that was? she wondered.

'I'll start at the beginning, shall I?' he asked, and she replied, with a stab at humour,

'OK. I never realised I would be settling down to a story, though.' She waited for him to return her weak smile but he didn't. He looked very serious.

'Do you remember the last time I visited you in a hospital?'

Lisa nodded. Remember? How could she ever forget? Hadn't it changed the entire course of her life? Changed *her*? Released some wild, free bird inside her which she had never thought even existed?

'Well, I never thought that I was opening a door inside me which I would then find impossible to shut.'

A little flare of hope rose inside her. Had he felt that way as well? Because that was exactly how she had felt! She tried to stifle the rising hope. She was deeply in love with him but he had never once said that he loved her, not even in their moment of passion when declarations of love should have been uttered with abandoned ease.

'You intrigued me.' He shot her a brooding, accusatory look.

'Is this a story or a fairy tale, Angus?' she asked, looking at him intently, trying to read the meaning behind his words.

'No interruptions. It's hard enough for me to say these words without interruptions. The fact is that I had never met a woman like you in my life before. You were such a confused mixture of contradictions. Intelligent, amusing, apologetic, without a shred of vanity. I left that hospital never expecting that I wouldn't be able to put you out of my mind, but I couldn't.

'Heaven only knows what I would have done if you had turned down that holiday. Hounded you to your lair, I expect. And I think now, that at the back of my mind I arranged the holiday with you in mind.'

It was an effort not to let every word send her higher and higher. There was a sheepish huskiness in his voice that made her head swim with a thousand possibilities.

'I really thought that I would get you out of my system if I saw you for more than a few hours. I really imagined that all that holiday would entail would be my showing you a good time. You were ripe for being shown a good time, Lisa. You probably don't realise how much. Those timid eyes, that defensive, vulnerable

face...you were begging to see things you'd never seen
before and I hadn't admitted it to myself, but I wanted
to be the one to show you sights that would make your
head spin. I had no idea that in the process I would also
end up wanting to show you more. Much, much more.'

Lisa felt a quiver of excitement. What was he telling
her, though? Just that he had been attracted to her. Then.
Once. No more than that.

'I don't know whether I told myself that you were a
challenge. I only knew that I was fiercely attracted to
you.' He looked at her very directly when he said this
and she met his eyes without blinking.

'Yes, I know,' she said quietly. They had both been
burning up with a desire that had taken them by surprise.
She looked across to the cot and wondered whether he
would have turned his back on that particular challenge
if he had only known what the outcome of yielding to
it would be.

'I noticed everything about you on that cruise. My
eyes followed you; they saw everything you did, every
move you made. I wanted to get inside your head so that
I could see what you were thinking as well. But that
wasn't easy. One step forward, two steps backwards.
You have no idea what a frustrating person you can be
without even trying! You would reveal so much but then
no more and I thought I was going to go mad trying to
get to the bottom of you. Then we made love and you
informed me that you wanted nothing more to do with
me.'

'I explained why,' Lisa said defensively, and he
smiled at her.

'Yes, you did. I thought you were a fool. I was offering you what I had never offered any other woman in

my life before, and you wanted no part of it. I could have strangled you, but in the end pride won out and I let you run away. I told myself that it wouldn't have lasted. I told myself that it would be better if you weren't around anyway, that my head would be clearer, that all I wanted from life was the satisfaction derived from work. That women, in the end, demanded complicated things which I had no intention of giving them. I knew that you were after marriage and marriage was just not on the agenda as far as I was concerned.'

'Then you found out that I was pregnant.'

'Then I found out that you were pregnant.'

'You weren't very happy.'

'I wasn't unhappy about the pregnancy. In fact, I was amazed at how calmly I accepted that. No, I was furious with you. Furious that you hadn't thought to get in touch with me.'

'Even though, if I had, you would have immediately accused me of being a gold-digger.'

'Being near you does nothing for my sanity,' he said ruefully, with a crooked smile. 'Then you had the nerve to inform me that you weren't going to marry me. I produced the most infallible arguments in the world and you turned your back and told me that I was wasting my time.'

'I changed my mind,' Lisa said, looking at him. 'I went to the cottage because I told myself that I needed to think things over, but I had already made up my mind to accept your proposal.'

'Which brings me to my last condition.'

Lisa was no longer feeling nervous. She didn't know what this last condition was, and her emotions were in a complete muddle, but there was something in his eyes,

something in the set of his features that made her feel
wonderfully reckless, even if she couldn't quite analyse
what that something was.

'You know what I'm telling you, don't you?' He
leaned a little over her. 'I'm in love with you, Lisa, and
it's no good marrying me for practical reasons if you
can't see your way to returning my love at some point
in time.'

She smiled. A smile that grew until it reflected the
happiness spreading through every tiny niche in her soul.

'About time,' she said, flinging her arms around his
neck. 'It's about time this love of mine was returned.'

Lisa and Angus stood outside the black and white house.
They had left Emily in London, with the girl who came
in from time to time to help out.

The garden was a mass of weeds, which appeared to
be winning the battle for supremacy over the rose bushes
and various other plants which had not been tended, ac-
cording to the estate agent, for a year and a half.

'Well, Mrs. Hamilton?' Angus slipped his arm round
her shoulders and she felt a thrill of pleasure, contentment, possession. They had been married now for six
months and she still loved the way he looked at her, the
way he excited her.

They let themselves into the cottage. It was musty,
but not dirty. Sunlight filtered through the uncurtained
windows, great shafts of it, like arrows striking the floor
and the walls.

'It has character,' Lisa said, looking around her.

'As well as all the necessary physical credentials.'

'In need of a face-lift, though.'

'Minor cosmetic surgery.'

They went upstairs and explored the bedrooms—all seven of them. The master bedroom overlooked an expanse of trees and garden and beyond that fields.

'Could you put down roots here?' he asked as she perched on the window-ledge and he placed his hands on either side of her. She never doubted his love for her, but in some tiny part of her she continued to be amazed that a man as sexy and as accomplished as he was could find her so utterly bewitching.

'I think I could,' Lisa said slowly. Putting down roots. With the man she loved and their child. The stuff that dreams were made of. She wrapped her arms around him and lifted her face to his, closing her eyes as his mouth parted her lips and explored wetly and hungrily.

When he slipped his hand under her shirt and caressed the swell of her breast, without the constraint of a bra because it was so warm a day, she giggled and protested half-heartedly and he grinned and buried his head into her neck, nipping with his teeth, rousing her with his fingers, which stroked and teased her swollen nipple.

He unbuttoned the shirt and drew it aside, then bent to suckle at her breasts, and then, on his knees, he lowered her jeans and she stepped out of them. His mouth trailed along her stomach, down to the furry patch of her womanhood. He nuzzled against it, and she groaned as his tongue began a delicate, leisurely exploration. She sat on the ledge of the bay window, parted her legs to accommodate his questing tongue and looked down hungrily at the dark head moving there.

How sweet the memory was of that first time, on that beach a thousand years ago. They had been back there, on their honeymoon, and had taken Emily to the same spot, and had felt the same wonder at the life they had created there.

She drew him up to her and said, with a flushed smile, 'I need you.'

'I should think so.' He unbuckled his belt and removed his trousers then pulled her onto him, and, with her legs wrapped round him, their bodies fused in wild passion. Her breasts pressed against his chest, her head was flung back and his mouth caressed her flesh—hot kisses that made her dizzy with desire and need.

As the roar in her veins gradually subsided, he said, half joking, half serious, 'Now this house is ours. We've christened it.'

'You're a corrupting influence, Angus Hamilton,' she said, laughing, slipping back into her clothes.

'Only with you, my darling.' He took her hand and they went down the stairs and out into the sunshine. 'I was made just for you and no one else.'

'Good.' Her voice was teasing, satisfied.

They stood outside and looked back at the house. Their house. The house of her dreams, even though, as she now knew, it mattered not in the least where they were, because wherever he was would be home.

HARLEQUIN  PRESENTS®

More heartwarming romances that feature fantastic men who *eventually* make fabulous fathers. Ready or not...

August 1997—
YESTERDAY'S BRIDE (#1903)
by Alison Kelly

September 1997—
ACCIDENTAL MISTRESS (#1909)
by Cathy Williams

October 1997—
THE PRICE OF A WIFE (#1914)
by Helen Brooks

FROM HERE TO PATERNITY—
men who find their way to fatherhood
by fair means, by foul, or even by default!

Available wherever Harlequin books are sold.

Look us up on-line at: http://www.romance.net   FHTP-397

Take 4 bestselling love stories FREE

Plus get a FREE surprise gift!

Special Limited-time Offer

Mail to Harlequin Reader Service®

3010 Walden Avenue
P.O. Box 1867
Buffalo, N.Y. 14240-1867

YES! Please send me 4 free Harlequin Presents® novels and my free surprise gift. Then send me 6 brand-new novels every month, which I will receive months before they appear in bookstores. Bill me at the low price of $2.90 each plus 25¢ delivery and applicable sales tax, if any*. That's the complete price and a savings of over 10% off the cover prices—quite a bargain! I understand that accepting the books and gift places me under no obligation ever to buy any books. I can always return a shipment and cancel at any time. Even if I never buy another book from Harlequin, the 4 free books and the surprise gift are mine to keep forever.

106 BPA A3UL

Name	(PLEASE PRINT)	
Address	Apt. No.	
City	State	Zip

This offer is limited to one order per household and not valid to present Harlequin Presents® subscribers. *Terms and prices are subject to change without notice. Sales tax applicable in N.Y.

UPRES-696   ©1990 Harlequin Enterprises Limited

Let's Celebrate!

LOVE & LAUGHTER™

invites you to
the party of the season!

Grab your popcorn and be prepared to laugh as we celebrate with **LOVE & LAUGHTER**.

Harlequin's newest series is going Hollywood!

Let us make you laugh with three months of terrific books, authors and romance, plus a chance to win a FREE 15-copy video collection of the best romantic comedies ever made.

For more details look in the back pages of any Love & Laughter title, from July to September, at your favorite retail outlet.

Don't forget the popcorn!

Available wherever
Harlequin books are sold.

 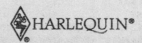HARLEQUIN®

Look us up on-line at: http://www.romance.net

LLCELEB

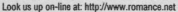

As Seen on TV!

Free Gift Offer

With a Free Gift proof-of-purchase
from any Harlequin® book, you can receive
a beautiful cubic zirconia pendant.

This stunning marquise-shaped stone is a genuine cubic
zirconia—accented by an 18" gold tone necklace.
(Approximate retail value $19.95)

Send for yours today...
compliments of ◈HARLEQUIN®

To receive your free gift, a cubic zirconia pendant, send us one original proof-of-purchase, photocopies not accepted, from the back of any Harlequin Romance®, Harlequin Presents®, Harlequin Temptation®, Harlequin Superromance®, Harlequin Intrigue®, Harlequin American Romance®, or Harlequin Historicals® title available at your favorite retail outlet, together with the Free Gift Certificate, plus a check or money order for $1.65 U.S./$2.15 CAN. (do not send cash) to cover postage and handling, payable to Harlequin Free Gift Offer. We will send you the specified gift. Allow 6 to 8 weeks for delivery. Offer good until December 31, 1997, or while quantities last. Offer valid in the U.S. and Canada only.

Free Gift Certificate

Name: _____

Address: _____

City: _____ State/Province: _____ Zip/Postal Code: _____

Mail this certificate, one proof-of-purchase and a check or money order for postage and handling to: HARLEQUIN FREE GIFT OFFER 1997. In the U.S.: 3010 Walden Avenue, P.O. Box 9071, Buffalo NY 14269-9057. In Canada: P.O. Box 604, Fort Erie, Ontario L2Z 5X3.

FREE GIFT OFFER   084-KEZ
ONE PROOF-OF-PURCHASE
To collect your fabulous FREE GIFT, a cubic zirconia pendant, you must include this original proof-of-purchase for each gift with the properly completed Free Gift Certificate.

084-KEZR

HARLEQUIN WOMEN KNOW ROMANCE WHEN THEY SEE IT.

And they'll see it on **ROMANCE CLASSICS**, the new 24-hour TV channel devoted to romantic movies and original programs like the special **Romantically Speaking—Harlequin™ Goes Prime Time**.

Romantically Speaking—Harlequin™ Goes Prime Time introduces you to many of your favorite romance authors in a program developed exclusively for Harlequin™ readers.

Watch for **Romantically Speaking—Harlequin™ Goes Prime Time** beginning in the summer of 1997.

If you're not receiving ROMANCE CLASSICS, call your local cable operator or satellite provider and ask for it today!

Escape to the network of your dreams.

See Ingrid Bergman and Gregory Peck in *Spellbound* on Romance Classics.

©1997 American Movie Classics Co. "Romance Classics" is a service mark of American Movie Classics Co. ® and ™ are trademarks of Harlequin Enterprises Ltd.

RMCLS-R2

Don't miss these Harlequin favorites by some of our most popular authors! And now you can receive a discount by ordering two or more titles!

		U.S.	CAN.
HT#25700	HOLDING OUT FOR A HERO by Vicki Lewis Thompson	$3.50 U.S. ☐	$3.99 CAN. ☐
HT#25699	WICKED WAYS by Kate Hoffmann	$3.50 U.S. ☐	$3.99 CAN. ☐
HP#11845	RELATIVE SINS by Anne Mather	$3.50 U.S. ☐	$3.99 CAN. ☐
HP#11849	A KISS TO REMEMBER by Miranda Lee	$3.50 U.S. ☐	$3.99 CAN. ☐
HR#03359	FAITH, HOPE AND MARRIAGE by Emma Goldrick	$2.99 U.S. ☐	$3.50 CAN. ☐
HR#03433	TEMPORARY HUSBAND by Day Leclaire	$3.25 U.S. ☐	$3.75 CAN. ☐
HS#70679	QUEEN OF THE DIXIE DRIVE-IN by Peg Sutherland	$3.99 U.S. ☐	$4.50 CAN. ☐
HS#70712	SUGAR BABY by Karen Young	$3.99 U.S. ☐	$4.50 CAN. ☐
HI#22319	BREATHLESS by Carly Bishop	$3.50 U.S. ☐	$3.99 CAN. ☐
HI#22335	BEAUTY VS. THE BEAST by M.J. Rodgers	$3.50 U.S. ☐	$3.99 CAN. ☐
AR#16577	BRIDE OF THE BADLANDS by Jule McBride	$3.50 U.S. ☐	$3.99 CAN. ☐
AR#16656	RED-HOT RANCHMAN by Victoria Pade	$3.75 U.S. ☐	$4.25 CAN. ☐
HH#28868	THE SAXON by Margaret Moore	$4.50 U.S. ☐	$4.99 CAN. ☐
HH#28893	UNICORN VENGEANCE by Claire Delacroix	$4.50 U.S. ☐	$4.99 CAN. ☐

(limited quantities available on certain titles)

	TOTAL AMOUNT	$ _____
DEDUCT:	10% DISCOUNT FOR 2+ BOOKS	$ _____
	POSTAGE & HANDLING	$ _____
	($1.00 for one book, 50¢ for each additional)	
	APPLICABLE TAXES*	$ _____
	TOTAL PAYABLE	$ _____
	(check or money order—please do not send cash)	

To order, complete this form, along with a check or money order for the total above, payable to Harlequin Books, to: **In the U.S.:** 3010 Walden Avenue, P.O. Box 9047, Buffalo, NY 14269-9047; **In Canada:** P.O. Box 613, Fort Erie, Ontario, L2A 5X3.

Name: _____

Address: _____ City: _____

State/Prov.: _____ Zip/Postal Code: _____

*New York residents remit applicable sales taxes.
Canadian residents remit applicable GST and provincial taxes.

Look us up on-line at: http://www.romance.net

HBKJS97